# The Duke and the Widow

## CHRISTINA DIANE

CHRISTINA
DIANE

The Duke and the Widow

Unlikely Betrothal Series

Copyright 2025 by Christina Diane

Edited by Emily Lawrence at Lawrence Editing

Cover Design by Erin at EDH Professionals

Beta Ready by Rachel Word



eBook ISBN: 978-1-964713-06-9

Paperback ISBN: 978-1-964713-14-4

# Contents

# Dedication

Dedicated to those who have suffered loss and continue
to move towards happiness.

# Note to Readers

Thank you so much for picking up my book—I'm truly delighted (and doing an undignified happy dance) that you're here!

Before we step into the historical world of Christina Diane, I wanted to share a little something about what to expect. While my books are set in the Regency era, I write with the modern reader in mind. You can expect stories that are character-driven, fast-paced, and heavy on the spice, with lively dialogue and plenty of heart.

I do my best to capture the setting and language of the time through research, but strict historical accuracy isn't my primary goal. Sometimes my characters insist on doing and speaking things their own way—and I let them. So, if you're looking for meticulous period detail and perfect historical precision, this book may not be what you are looking for (and that's completely okay!).

But if you're here for passionate heroines, swoonworthy gentlemen, witty banter, high stakes, high heat, and happily ever afters, all wrapped in a Regency-inspired world that welcomes diverse, bold, and intriguing characters—you're in the right place.

I hope this story sweeps you off your feet and carries you into a world of romance, tension, and a touch of scandal.

Much love and swoon,

# Content Warnings

This book doesn't dive deep into the dark stuff—but I do recommend checking the content warnings on this book if you have trauma from lost loves ones. You might also encounter boundary-challenged relatives, oversharing friends, and a generous dash of spice. I aim to flag anything that might need a warning, but if I miss something, send me a message so I can update the list for future readers. To keep this message spoiler-free, you can check out identified content warnings here: https://christinadianebooks.com/content-warnings/

# Chapter 1

## KENT, ENGLAND - JULY 1810

Rosina held her husband's hand, thinking back on the short, loving marriage they had shared thus far. It was unfathomable that illness could reduce such a strong, virile man to skin and bones. She would have given anything for some sort of miracle to bring him back to her. She pleaded to the skies every night for the last couple of months for some sign of improvement and any assistance from some other force that would make him well again.

"Do you remember our wedding breakfast?" His voice was frail compared to the confident baritone he had always possessed.

She rubbed her thumb over his hand. "Of course, my love. Some of my family is still quite scandalized, you know." She laughed, recalling the memory of the unexplainable grass stains on the back of her dress and the twigs in her hair. They had been so ready to consummate their marriage—not that it was the first time they had been intimate—that they thought they could slip to the gardens for a quick tryst and took a bit of a tumble.

He opened his eyes and looked at her. All the love he'd had for her on that day still shone there, and she fought not to let him see her cry. He needed to preserve his strength, so he might have a chance of overcoming whatever it was that ailed him. As foolish as she was to continue to hope. The doctors didn't know exactly what it was, but in the similar cases they had seen, the patients hadn't survived.

"I'm lucky to have been able to love you for the time we've had," he said.

They had been married for almost two years, but they had loved each other since their youth. Ryan, Marquess Preston, had been her older brother's best friend, and she'd followed them around everywhere. The boys were only a year older than her, and she made them let her go fishing and climb trees. She had always been a force to be reckoned with, and they didn't dare tell her no.

"I want us to go visit our spot in the woods at my father's estate," she said.

He coughed and smiled at her. The memory of the first time Ry had kissed her had always been one of their favorites. Rosina had been three-and-ten, while he was four-and-ten, and they were playing a game of hide-and-seek with her brother, even if admittedly they were a bit old to be doing so. They found a place in the woods where the trees formed an enclosure that they could just squeeze into. Pressed against each other, trying to quiet their ragged breathing from running through the woods, they stared into each other's eyes, and something happened. And she saw him differently than she had before. It appeared to have been the same for him because he leaned down and pressed a soft kiss against her lips. Her heart had belonged to him ever since.

"I was so nervous," he said. "I wasn't certain if you might slap me."

"When you are well, we shall go back there, and I will be the one to kiss you."

A frown formed on his handsome face. His features were gaunt, but she still saw the man she married.

"My Rose, you must accept what is happening. I will not survive this, and I must know that you are going to be all right when I am gone."

No longer able to control the tears, she allowed a few to escape down her cheeks. She used her free hand to brush back the sandy brown hair from his forehead. "We mustn't give up hope, Ry."

He patted the bed beside him, and she moved to settle in with him. He wrapped his once-muscular arm around her and she leaned against him. His body felt different, but he was still her Ry.

He married her before she even had a come out. His parents had been worried that a man of nine-and-ten needed to sow his wild oats, but he informed anyone who dared to question his love for her that his mind would never be changed. Ry convinced her father he was prepared to take up his responsibilities and provide for her. He forwent university and dove into learning about estate management at their country home, becoming every bit the marquess he was expected to be. He would be a duke one day, or he should be. Her heart splintered as she had never imagined that her beloved husband might pass before his father.

"You are going to have to go on without me soon enough, Rose," he said, pressing his sallow cheek to the top of her head.

They had been each other's first everything. Neither of them had even kissed another. Even when Ry was away at Eton, he remained true to her in every way. When she was six-and-ten, they began exploring each other's bodies. They had learnt everything about obtaining their pleasure together, with nary an inch that hadn't been touched, kissed, explored, or tasted time and time again. Their coupling had always been untamed and fiery, and then afterwards their embrace was tender and affectionate.

"I can't," she said, sobbing into his chest. "I can't lose you."

He rubbed her back, the same way he had for years, and she cried harder.

"You must, sweetheart. I want you to have a full life. You deserve love, laughter, and children. You are going to make the most amazing mother." His voice caught on the last word, and she hugged him tighter.

"I need you, Ry," she said, wiping her eyes and looking up at him.

He sighed. "I know, my love. If love were enough to heal me, I would live forever here with you, Rose."

He coughed again and laid his head back on the pillow, needing frequent naps the weaker he became. She lay with him in silence, willing the sickness to leave his body. Making every promise she could think of to whoever might hear her that she would give her very soul if it would allow Ry to grow old with her.

*Two months later*

Rosina's brother, John, kept his arm around her shoulders as they watched the casket being lowered into the ground. Her family and Ry's had tried to talk her out of attending the funeral as women didn't do so. But she sobbed and went into such hysterics that they relented and allowed her to attend.

She had been with him almost every moment for the last couple of months, and she was beside the bed, holding his hand, when he took his last breath. She owed it to him to be there. But she wasn't certain how she would keep breathing once the dirt covered him and the only thing left of him was a headstone and the memories she carried of him in her shattered heart.

She moved as if she might step forward, and her brother tightened his hold on her shoulder. Part of her wanted to throw herself on the casket and go with him, but she knew it wasn't what he would have wanted. He wanted her to have a life and to go on without him, but she still couldn't fathom how she could be expected to do so.

After the funeral, they returned to the house she had shared with Ry. His brother, Rich, had become the marquess upon Ry's passing, but he was only eight-and-ten and intended to attend Cambridge before he took up his responsibilities.

As if she hadn't even been in the room, both families talked about her life and where she would live. They decided she could remain in the house as long as she wished since Rich wouldn't take up residence. She stared at the wall and did her best to ignore the conversation that only further solidified that nothing about her life would ever be the same again.

When the exhaustion of the day consumed her, she trudged upstairs and, out of habit, went straight to the bedchamber she had shared with Ry. They never spent a single night apart in their home, even the times when she slept in a chair by the bed. The sheets had been freshly changed and the bed turned down, but she couldn't bring herself to cross the threshold into the room.

She turned on her heel and went to the marchioness' chamber. Until then, it had only served as a dressing room and a place to keep her clothing. Rosina didn't bother to ring for her maid or to remove the black dress she wore. She kicked off her shoes and climbed into the bed, then hugged the pillow to her body.

Rosina wasn't sure how she was expected to go on in a world where Ry wasn't. She closed her eyes, longing for sleep, the only place where she might see him again.

# Chapter 2

## NORFOLK, ENGLAND - SEPTEMBER 1813

"**A**nd who are you staring at?" Lily asked, tugging Rosina's attention away from the man who had entered the salon. She and her friend were guests at a country house party hosted by Lord and Lady Ockham. Ry had been friends with Lord Ockham and a few of the other gentlemen in attendance when they were at Eton, and he had visited her after Ry's passing to pay his respects.

The party had around thirty guests, all members of the ton. Their hosts went all out since they missed the events of the London season because of the birth of their first child. House parties proved to create many opportunities to indulge in carnal pursuits if one navigated them properly, and finding a gentleman to bring to her bed was an option she would consider as part of the activities for the fortnight they were in attendance.

"That is the Duke of St. Albans," Rosina replied. The man was devastatingly handsome with his dark, almost black hair and broad-shouldered, taut form.

"You seem taken with him," Lily said, giving her a knowing look.

That couldn't be further from the truth. At least not for anything beyond how he might perform in the bedchamber. It had been almost three years since Ry had passed, and she still didn't believe she could ever allow herself to care for another man in the way she had for her husband. After two years had passed, she'd desired the physical aspects of being with a man, and she'd felt so guilty that she locked herself in her chamber for two weeks.

After replaying some of her last conversations with Ry, she convinced herself she could do so and keep feelings out of it. Men did so all the time, so surely she could as well. The first time had been awkward, and she went home and cried herself to sleep. But she had also felt something again, something besides grief, even if only for a little while, and decided she would entertain the gentleman again.

The man decided he wanted to marry her after they had several trysts, and when she refused him, he spread it around that she was an easy mark for the men of the ton. It damaged her reputation in some circles, but she still had her close friends, and after a break from the company of gentlemen while the gossip ran its course, she pursued another partner.

In reality, she had only had a few partners, regardless of what some sets in society believed. She never intended to marry again, so if the reputation kept marriage-minded men away, she would be all the better for it.

"This is his first event in society," Rosina said, "other than casual appearances, where his attendance was required. He would make an intriguing friend."

"Intriguing, indeed."

Rosina jerked her head towards her friend, planning to say something smart, but their hostess approached.

"Are you both having a good time so far? Dinner should be announced soon," Lady Ockham said.

"We are, my lady," Rosina said. "Lily and I hoped you might introduce us to Lord Knox. We aren't certain who he is."

Their hostess nodded in understanding. "I believe I heard something about him courting Lady Lily," she said, giving Lily a kind smile.

"At least that is what my father's intentions are," Lily replied, the irritation evident in her tone. Rosina's friend had been considered a wallflower when she made her come out earlier in the season, and her father had taken matters into his own hands in his mission to see her wed to a titled peer.

"Well, come with me," Lady Ockham said. "I think I see him among some of the other guests. You probably couldn't see him from here."

The ladies followed their hostess, moving through a group of guests until they reached a gentleman standing near the sideboard.

"Lord Knox," their hostess started, "Please allow me to introduce Lady Lily and Lady Preston."

"My ladies," he said, bowing to them. "Pleased to meet you both."

The man took Lily's hand in his. "I hope you might allow me to spend some time in your presence over the next fortnight."

"We shall let you two get acquainted," Lady Ockham said, looping her arm in Rosina's. "Perhaps we will see a betrothal by the end of the house party," she continued, leaning close so only Rosina could hear her. "It's the hope of any hostess and just might make up for missing the season."

"I hope you get your wish," Rosina said, becoming more aware that they were approaching the same group as the Duke of St. Albans.

"Your Grace, my lords," Lady Ockham started, "have you all met Lady Preston?"

She was already acquainted with Lord Onslow and Lord Camden, so they just gave her a quick bow.

"I don't believe we have been introduced, my lady," the duke said. His voice did things to her. It was deeper than she had expected, especially given that he was around her age.

"Lady Preston, meet His Grace, the Duke of St. Alban's," Lady Ockham said.

He took her hand in his, and he stirred something in her insides. She brushed off the reaction as purely physical as it would appear by the look of him that he would indeed suit her tastes. His tall, taut form was enough to make any woman swoon, aside from her. She would never swoon. "Pleased to meet you, my lady."

She didn't have a doubt in her mind he was likely the one she would select to enjoy the fortnight with, if he were amenable, and as long as he didn't do something idiotic like tell her he was looking for his perfect duchess or some other nonsense.

"You as well, Your Grace. It is good to have you join us."

She glanced to each side and noticed that the rest of the group had left them alone, moving on to other conversations.

"I only hope my manners are passable, given that I have spent little time out in society."

She grinned at him. "Well, even if they aren't, no one shall correct you. Given that you are a duke."

He shrugged, with every bit of the haughty air that one would expect from a duke. "Then can I count on you to tell me so?"

She gave him an overdramatic fake curtsy. "If that is what my duke commands."

He stiffened his shoulders and took an even stuffier stance than before. "It is." Then he flashed her a wide grin.

The man was too handsome for his own good. Up close, she could tell his dark hair was certain to be silky to the touch. He caught her gaze, and his piercing light blue eyes were even more intense set against his dark, chiseled features. He was all hard lines, and the shadows from the candlelit room made him appear almost dangerous, even though she already knew better from their brief banter.

His finely tailored evening kit left little to the imagination regarding how rippled his muscles might be beneath his clothing. He wasn't one of the gentlemen who had to add padding to his garments to fill out his breeches and coats.

The Duke of St. Albans was everything she wanted in a short-term bed partner, as long as he wasn't in attendance to take a bride. Hopefully, since he was a tad on the young side to consider marriage, luck would be on her side.

"What made you decide to join us for the coming fortnight, Your Grace? It hasn't gone unnoticed that you haven't attended many society events and have never attended a season."

He raised his chin, and the intensity of his gaze caused heat to pool between her thighs. He was going to drive her to distraction, to be certain.

"I came here to meet you, my lady."

She choked on nothing but air. Once she recovered, she replied, "Excuse me. What did you just say?"

He took a step closer so there was only a matter of inches between their bodies. "I believe our interests may align if what I have heard about you is true."

It occurred to her that she should be offended, but from the way he looked at her, she couldn't help but be more than a bit intrigued. "And what interests might those be?"

"The pleasurable kind," he said, lowering his voice and clasping his hands behind his back.

Her thighs were damp, and she could already imagine what he would look like naked in her bed. "I guess we shall see if you meet my requirements."

"And what are those?"

Dinner was announced, and she shifted her attention to the rest of the room. She was almost certain that if anyone noticed her talking to the duke, that they would assume they would be friendly while at the house party. She laughed to herself because they may very well be correct in their assumption.

"My lady?" He extended his arm to her to escort her to dinner.

She clasped it and the feel of his bicep confirmed her assumptions about what he might look like without all the layers of clothing that separated her from her prize.

"Are you going to answer my question?" he asked, leaning towards her, his hot breath warming the top of her ear.

"In due time, Your Grace." She glanced up at him and smirked. She may want to explore such an arrangement with him, but she couldn't make it easy for the man. Even a duke must work for things now and then.

# Chapter 3

James Talbot, Duke of St. Albans, had come to the Ockham house party for one reason, and one reason only. To meet the beautiful widow he had heard about from one of his friends and see if she might invite him to her bed. He had doubted if he made the right choice in attending at all, given that he wasn't that thrilled about being at a society event.

His responsibilities kept him from attending many events, and he had grown accustomed to being at home with his younger brothers. Since their parents had passed, he was all they had. They were a small, unconventional family, but they had made things work. He was as much a father to them as he was a brother, and he always had to set the example they needed.

With his brothers at Eton until the holiday break, he had the chance to do something for himself. Both of his parents had passed away by the time he was of the legal age of one-and-twenty, but his father needed constant care for almost two years prior to that. He'd had to take up the responsibilities of the dukedom while his father was confined to his bed, while also overseeing the care of his parents and his little twin brothers. The boys were but eight years old when their mother died, and then were the age of ten by the time the duke had succumbed to his injuries.

The day his father died, James couldn't decide if he should weep or be glad for the man. His father had missed their mother daily for the last two years and frequently called out to her in his sleep when the medications made his mind foggy. There were several times when James had to remind his father of the events that had claimed her life and watch as his father's heart broke all over again.

James wasn't certain he wished to encounter such heartbreak, thus he had decided he may never wed. Or if he did, it would be many years away and only to produce the expected heir. But perhaps if one of his brothers wed one day and had children, the title would just pass to one of them. He had years before he would even have to make such a decision because he would never wed while his brothers were still in his care. They needed him.

They needed his full attention, and he couldn't introduce someone who might disrupt the peace they had finally found with just the three of them.

But with the boys at Eton, James might ease the tension that had been growing within him for some time. He was still a man, after all, and he had constant urges to sate his needs and finally bed a woman. His few friends from his school days would have a hearty laugh at his expense if they knew the Duke of St. Albans was an untouched virgin. They'd probably insist he go with them immediately to the nearest brothel and take care of matters then and there.

He always listened to the stories of their conquests and laughed and taunted when the other men did, then groaned internally, knowing that his own fist around his cock was the only attention he would receive.

James had been tempted several times to venture to a brothel as he knew his friends would encourage him to do so, but he always considered the example he wished to set for his brothers. Maintaining the image of the perfect gentleman for the sake of the boys constantly nagged at him.

Although the urges to partake in the appetites of the flesh had grown stronger. James had been on the cusp of caving and attending a brothel a few towns over until one of his friends mentioned the beautiful widow who didn't wish to wed. As luck would have it, he found himself invited to a house party where she would be in attendance, and the opportunity seemed too perfect to pass up.

He could appear in society without the need to bore himself with London ballrooms and eager debutantes, and if all went as planned, he'd spend his nights warming a certain lady's bed and curbing desires that his hand barely satisfied any longer.

She might even be open to an ongoing arrangement with the required discretion if all went well.

When he finally met her, beautiful didn't seem to be a strong enough word. She was radiant, alluring, tempting, and any other adjective that a poet might come up with to describe such a lovely woman. Her blond hair was almost golden in the low lighting, and a couple of stray curls perfectly framed her heart-shaped face.

Catching her gaze for the first time, she had eyes that looked almost like perfect emeralds, beautiful and tinted with a hint of mischief. His cock fought against the hold of his breeches when she smirked at him. She had already tempted him more than he could have imagined, and he knew he must figure out what she needed to entertain an arrangement with him.

He would do anything just short of scandal or marriage. Some might believe bedding her at all would be scandalous, but with him as a duke and her as a willing widow, they would be afforded the courtesy of most turning a blind eye, so long as they did nothing too obvious.

When she gripped his arm, the touch—even through his clothing—sent electricity running through him that did nothing to ease the ache he already had. It was to his benefit that he would be seated for a while as he'd need the meal to get his wits about him.

He seated her in her place. "I look forward to speaking with you again," he said, then leaned closer to her, "minx." She smelled like lilies, and the scent intoxicated his senses.

"You as well, Duke," she said, winking at him. It wasn't the proper way to address him, but he liked the way her lips formed the word and tried not to imagine the other ways he might view her lips.

He took his seat a few chairs down and across the table from her, pleased with himself. For a man with so little experience with women, it would seem he may just have a chance of winning over one of the most desired women of the ton. He only hoped he might earn an invitation to her chamber soon and not waste a single night of the time they could enjoy together.

The next morning, he set out to claim his prize, even more eager to do so than when he had first arrived. The previous evening hadn't moved things along as quickly as he had hoped. After dinner, he hadn't been able to get her alone. He'd been limited to glances from across the room, which didn't give him enough to know if she would be agreeable to him appearing in her chamber after everyone settled into their beds, or whoever's beds they intended to warm.

Frustrated by the anticipation, he took himself in hand before he attempted to sleep, hoping it might ease the tension that plagued his body. If nothing else, it aided in his ability to get a good night's rest. He woke up that morning ready to do what it took to gain a private audience with Lady Preston.

On the walk to the breakfast room, James wondered how his brothers fared away at Eton. Once they had turned twelve, it had been time for them to attend school. Anxious thoughts consumed him since he had been away from them and how they would do without him. At least they had each other. Their instructors were to inform him immediately if anything was amiss, but he hadn't heard a word. His staff would ensure correspondence reached him at the Ockhams', but he couldn't help but wonder what they were doing. And hopefully they were behaving themselves.

When he reached where the other guests had gathered to break their fast, he was sorely disappointed to find that Lady Preston had no open seats around her. He internally groaned and went to the sideboard to make his plate before settling into a chair at the other end of the table near their hosts.

He speared a piece of fruit and smoothed his chewing when he realized he was scowling far too much and didn't wish for anyone to ask him about his mood.

"I hope you are enjoying your time with us so far, Your Grace," Lady Ockham said, capturing his attention from staring at his plate.

"Very much so," he replied. It wasn't completely a lie. He intended to enjoy his time very much, so things could only start looking up from there, right?

"I hope you will join the Pall Mall game after breakfast," she continued. "I am sure the young ladies in attendance would enjoy the opportunity to partner with a duke."

He eyed her curiously. "Pall Mall is an individual game, is it not?"

Mirth flooded her ladyship's expression. "I have changed things a bit. We will have partners, with the pair sharing a mallet and ball, thus alternating swings when it is their turn."

Matchmaking attempts at its finest, from what he could tell. House parties were notorious for garnering a few proposals. Marriage was too rich for his blood, but he wouldn't mind a bit of help in his private matchmaking endeavor, of sorts.

"You can count me in as one of your willing players," he replied. If he could ensure he partnered with Lady Preston, he could spend the game at her side and determine her requirements.

His hostess grinned at him and then her husband escorted her away from the table, and she started encouraging guests to meet on the lawn after they finished. He ate the rest of his meal in silence, thinking about what he might say to the beautiful widow.

James followed the rest of the guests outside and joined the group that formed a circle around their hostess. He could not focus on the rules of the game as his eyes remained locked on Lady Preston. She was whispering with Lord Craven, an earl he'd met the previous evening. Her hand patted the man's arm when he spoke to her, and she gave him a wide grin. The entire exchange was far too familiar, and it irritated him.

As if she sensed his irritation, she caught his gaze before he could look away and flashed him that smirk that tempted him beyond measure. He needed to control his reaction to her, since it wouldn't do to pitch a tent in his breeches in the middle of the Pall Mall game.

Before he could attempt to claim her as a partner, she was already at the rack, selecting a mallet.

"I hope you won't mind purple, Nick, but it is my favorite color," she called out to Craven.

That she was on such an informal basis with the man, using his given name, didn't bode well for him, especially if she were thinking of taking the earl to her bed instead of him. He glanced around, realizing he had claimed no one to partner with, and noticed a young lady, Miss Stone, standing alone. Thankfully, he had been introduced to her after dinner the prior evening.

"Would you like to partner with me, Miss Stone?"

She looked up at him, and her eyes sparkled with delight. "Oh, very much so, Your Grace."

Just perfect. The chit was already setting her cap at him, planning their wedding, and imagining what their three children would look like.

James offered her a polite nod. "Why don't you select a mallet for us?"

She giggled, and he fought the urge to roll his eyes. Miss Stone sauntered up to the rack and selected the white mallet. She brandished it as if she wished for him to give some sign of approval. James offered a tight smile, and they moved to stand beside each other in line to await their turn.

Conveniently, he was standing beside Lady Preston. The alluring scent of lilies met his nostrils, and he knew it came from her. He leaned slightly towards her. "Good to see you this morning, minx."

"You as well, Duke," she whispered.

"Can we—" he started before the chit beside him interrupted.

"Your Grace, tell me all about your country home," Miss Stone said. When he glanced at her, she was staring daggers at Lady Preston, and when he glanced between them, it appeared that Lady Preston was highly amused by the turn of events.

"Don't let me keep you from your young lady," she whispered, muffling her laughter.

He did roll his eyes that time and then turned back to face the eager young chit. "Willowcrest is a beautiful estate. I prefer to spend most of my time there." His tone was a bit more clipped than he intended, but she didn't seem to notice or care.

Fortunately, it was their turn, so he motioned for her to take the first swing. She was an abysmal player and sent the ball past the first wicket. It was going to be a long morning, indeed. James glanced back at Lady Preston, who was setting up to take her swing. She was graceful in the way she moved, and her ball smoothly rolled right through the wicket. She caught his gaze and gave him a bit of a sympathetic grin.

"Your Grace," the chit beside him said, attempting to get his attention. "We must wait by our ball until our next turn."

"Oh, of course. Lead the way, Miss Stone."

The rest of the game was spent much the same way over the next few hours. He watched Lady Preston as often as he could, while Miss Stone tried to engage him in a one-sided conversation. It wasn't lost on James that the young miss attempted everything to catch his attention, hoping he might court her. He did his best to dissuade her of such a notion by keeping his distance from her when they awaited their turn and only engaging in light conversation.

Finally, Lord Irvine and Lady Eliza were declared the victors of the game, and he could vacate the presence of Miss Stone to seek an audience with Lady Preston. He breathed a sigh of relief when Craven left her side, but then a pretty, red-haired young lady with spectacles joined her side. Would he ever have the opportunity to speak with the lady alone again?

James stood there for a few moments, debating whether he would join their conversation, and his hesitation cost him dearly when the voice of his Pall Mall partner sounded behind him.

"Oh, Your Grace, I believe I am in need of assistance."

He cringed and then schooled his features before he turned around to face her.

"How might I help, Miss Stone?" His tone didn't convey his excitement to assist, but it was one occasion when he was thankful that his duke title afforded him the right to be haughty and no one would think twice about it. It wasn't a behavior he used often, but he was beyond annoyed.

"I believe I hurt my ankle. Might you help me back to the house?"

So that was what she was playing at.

"Of course." He stepped closer to her and put her arm around his shoulder so he could support her and help her walk.

"Ouch. I'm not certain I can walk."

The chit was unbelievable. He glanced around, hoping any other gentleman was nearby that he might pass her off to. The whole thing reminded him of why he avoided social events. The marriage-minded woman hoped to win the opportunity to become a duchess, and their aspirations erased all of their good sense.

Resigning himself to his fate, he spoke again through gritted teeth. "Will you allow me to carry you, then?"

"That would be most kind of you, Your Grace." She fluttered her eyelashes, and he looked away to keep from rolling his eyes directly in her face.

He scooped her up, and she made a show of wrapping her arms around his neck, holding him tighter than she ought. James quickened his pace, deciding that the faster he got her inside, the faster he might rid himself of her.

Once they entered the salon from the terrace, he deposited her on the nearest settee. "I shall fetch a maid to tend to you." His words were hurried, and he departed from her presence before she could ask any more of him. He knew the maid was wholly unnecessary since the chit had made the whole thing up, but he did as he said and told the first maid he found about the miss in need of assistance.

Avoiding the salon at all costs, he bypassed the room and exited to the terrace from a long hallway. For a moment, he thought it might have just been easier to just visit a brothel after all. But when he saw Lady Preston leaning to smell the bloom of a rose from the bushes that lined the grass around the terrace, something about her called to him. It became far easier to understand why seamen were lured to their deaths by the allure of a siren.

Her friend was still at her side, but he wouldn't allow anything else to keep him from engaging her in conversation. He descended the staircase from the terrace and approached them at the line of bushes. "My ladies, you both look lovely this morning."

The redhead gave him a knowing look, and he could only assume she was aware of her friend's reputation.

"Your Grace, have you been introduced to Lady Lily yet?" Lady Preston asked.

He took the lady's hand and bowed over it. "I haven't had the pleasure, but I am pleased to make your acquaintance, my lady."

"You as well, Your Grace," Lady Lily said.

"Do you know what our hostess has planned for us next?" he asked, including both ladies in his question.

"I believe a luncheon shall be set up on the terrace shortly," Lady Preston replied.

Before he could say anything else, Lord Knox approached, and James fought his irritation. If he were bested again in getting an audience with the woman of his desire, he might have to resort to throwing her over his shoulder.

"Lady Lily, might we go for a stroll in the gardens before luncheon?"

James almost released an audible sigh that his luck might finally change and he'd get the beauty alone.

"That would be lovely, my lord," she replied. She caught Lady Preston's attention. "Surely you will be all right on your own?" She posed it as a question, but by the way she smirked at her friend, it gave James the impression that it was more of a jest. Perhaps they had even discussed him, which might be a point in his favor.

"Of course," Lady Preston replied. "Have a pleasant stroll. I am sure His Grace will make for fine company."

The pair departed, finally leaving him alone with the only woman he wished to speak with. Before anyone else could approach, he took her hand and placed it in the crook of his arm, escorting her on a stroll in the yard, away from the other guests who still congregated under the tent set up for those who didn't partake in the game.

"My lady, I believe you owe me a list of requirements."

# Chapter 4

Rosina had to give the duke credit for his efforts. He had certainly worked hard to earn an audience with her. She found it amusing, especially when Miss Stone made such a show to get him to carry her back inside. The chit was certainly trying her hardest to snag a duke.

Rosina could tell the man was annoyed to no end by the situation, but he did what was expected of him, then was right back in her sphere, trying to catch her attention. It felt good to be pursued. Her other arrangements began because she selected the men and was the one to do the pursuing.

She found she enjoyed being chased a bit, almost as if she were being courted, which was a silly notion since she didn't wish for such nonsense. But she was still a woman, and she could admit that part of her longed to be desired and wanted, and that certainly seemed to be the case with the duke.

"Well, the first requirement is attraction, my dear duke." She grinned up at him as they continued on their slow stroll.

"And do I meet that requirement?" he asked, playing the part of the haughty duke.

"I suppose."

"Minx," he hissed. "I am willing to admit that you very much meet the requirement for me if you must know. What else?"

Even if she had suspected he found her attractive, a lady always relished hearing such things, especially from a man as handsome as the one beside her. And he was a duke, so women threw themselves at him, leaving him with plenty of options.

"I require discretion. Many may assume if you spend time in my company that we have an arrangement of sorts, but we need not confirm it for them. Let them wonder and assume."

"That would be a requirement for me as well, so I am in agreement."

"That brings us to the most important requirement. No talk of marriage." She glanced up at him to ascertain his reaction. "If you are seeking your duchess, I am not the woman for you to keep in your company. I have no desire to wed."

"It should seem we are on the same page in all things, my lady. I am most certainly not seeking a duchess, nor do I wish to wed for a very long time, if ever."

She smirked at him. "If you are truly agreeable to the arrangement, then you are welcome to sneak into my bedchamber, Duke."

He stopped walking and turned her to face him. "I have a couple of requirements of my own."

Well, perhaps the man would make things interesting.

"Go on, Your Grace," she said, nodding for him to continue.

"I won't make any grand gestures of love, nor do I expect anything from you, other than your sole attention."

She eyed him curiously. "What do you mean?"

"I mean that even men avoiding marriage don't wish to share the woman they take to bed. So if you have something going already with Craven, or any other gentleman, this won't work."

Rosina laughed. "Nick? Oh, my dear duke, I would never take up such a relationship with the man. Nor do I have any other arrangements." She paused to smirk at him. "So can I also assume you won't be sneaking off to alcoves with the simpering misses who are clamoring for your attention?"

"I told you already. I only came here for you," he replied, his eyes already consumed with desire. "So now that we have settled those terms, that brings me to my last requirement." He paused and drew a breath. "Even though our arrangement isn't one based on feelings, I still get to kiss you."

She couldn't help but lick her lips from thinking about kissing the man. She wasn't opposed to kissing as it would heighten the intensity of the wicked things they would do. "I hope you will use your mouth on me in many ways, Your Grace."

His breath hitched from her words, and she glanced at his crotch, catching sight of the large ridge that took shape. She glanced around and noted they were far away from the others and there was a tall row of bushes beside the house.

Rosina pushed him back against the side of the house, behind the cover of the bushes where she knew they wouldn't be seen, and pressed her hand against the bulge, gripping him. He certainly wouldn't disappoint. "Do you wish to kiss me now, Duke?"

He didn't speak and responded by pulling her against him and pressing his lips to hers. The electricity of their lips touching unleashed something inside of her, and she immediately opened to him and swept her tongue into his mouth. He seemed timid in the kiss, but she reasoned she had caught him off guard.

She tasted the tea on his breath from breakfast and massaged her tongue harder against his. Enjoying the low growls he released into their kiss, she pressed her body harder against his.

They couldn't continue much longer without the risk of someone coming upon them, and she was already going to be in a state of dissatisfaction until later that evening, when he visited her for the first time. She suckled his tongue and gave his bottom lip a light nip before she pulled away.

Placing her hand back into the crook of his arm, she pulled him away from the house so they strolled in the open again. "Does that mean you shall come tonight, Duke?" The double meaning in her words was completely intended, and she smirked at him.

"You must show me where your chamber is, minx. I am uncertain how I will wait until tonight."

She shrugged. "At least it shall be worth the wait."

"I have no doubt about that, my lady."

Rosina didn't doubt it either. She hadn't wanted a man as much as she wanted the one before her in a long time. The realization frightened her only for a moment until she reminded herself that it had been a bit since her last encounter and her body anticipated what she knew would await her that evening. If the size of his bulge in her hand was any indication, she was in for a thrilling evening, indeed.

Rosina separated herself from the duke after their stroll. Many of the guests would assume that they had become friendly, but it would be best to avoid constantly remaining in each other's company if they hoped to keep the rumor from spreading beyond the house party after they all departed at the end of the fortnight. She hoped that though the guests might suspect, they would long forget to spread the gossip once they returned home.

She had been seated near the man at dinner, which made it only proper that she engaged him in a bit of light conversation along with the other guests who sat nearby. It had been a pleasant meal, with lively conversation. One of the more enjoyable evenings she'd had in a long time, she realized. It surprised her how much she enjoyed speaking with him, and the surrounding guests, about all manner of topics.

After dinner, they all congregated in the salon, and she did her best to avoid ending up in the same groups with him. She had been successful at maintaining distance between them, but it didn't stop her from glancing at the man every chance she got. There was something charming about the handsome duke, and it affected her in ways that alarmed her. Not enough to change her mind about coupling with the man, but enough that she didn't wish to think any further about why she had such a reaction.

If she were honest with herself, she was nervous about his visit to her chamber later that evening. Her confidence in her prowess in the bedchamber was strong, yet she had an intense desire to please him more than she had with the other partners. Something she hadn't felt in a long time. Not since Ry. She closed her eyes and drew a steadying breath at the memory of her dear husband.

"Everything all right, my lady?" a rich baritone asked beside her. She glanced up at the duke and gave him a small grin.

"Have you changed your mind about our arrangement?" he asked, concern in his furrowed brow.

She shook off her previous thoughts. "No, Duke. Of course not. You recall which chamber is mine?"

"Take a left from the grand staircase and then the fourth door on the right," he whispered, his bottom lip brushing her ear. She shivered from the sensation that coursed through her body.

"You have a good memory."

"Well, you made me repeat it to you five times. Six, including that one."

She hid her laugh behind her hand. "Well, we can't have you stumbling into the chamber of some innocent miss. You'd have your duchess before the night was out."

He scanned the room, ensuring they would still go unheard. "How do I know you aren't tricking me and the directions aren't to your chamber?" His tone was one of jest, but perhaps just a slight undertone of concern that she might play such a trick on him.

"You will just have to sneak in tonight and see who you shall find waiting, Duke." She winked at him. "On that note, I believe I am headed for my bed this evening. I do hope you have a good night, Your Grace."

Rosina caught Lily's eye and nodded towards the door. Lily understood her meeting and said something to Lord Knox, then joined Rosina's side. Rosina looped her arm through Lily's, and they set off towards the staircase.

"What do you think of Lord Knox so far?" Rosina asked once they were out of earshot from the other guests.

There was something hesitant in Lily's expression. "I'm not certain. He appears to be a kind man. I shall need more time to better ascertain his character."

"You have many more days to spend in his presence. I am certain you will know your mind on the matter soon."

Lily sighed. "I don't think it matters anyway since my father is the one making the arrangements."

"Your father shouldn't force you to marry someone to further his own standing," Rosina ground out. She would give Lily's father a piece of her mind if it came to it. Her mother, too.

"Enough about that," Lily said. "Tell me about the duke. I assume he is to be your…friend…for the duration of the house party?"

Rosina's cheeks heated, and she wasn't certain why. She wasn't the type of woman to blush at the thought of a man. "You are correct. We are aligned with what we seek from each other."

"I hope he is everything and more," Lily said, then nudged Rosina with her shoulder. "Perhaps I'll know one day what it is to have such experiences."

They reached the top of the staircase and took the left towards their chambers.

"Indeed, you shall. Just remember what I told you the night we met. Only one man shall matter."

When they reached Lily's door, the third door on the right, Lily clasped both of Rosina's hands in hers. "You seem to believe in love for everyone but yourself."

She squeezed Lily's hands. "I've already had my love, and that part of myself died and was buried in the cold dirt with him." Rosina tamped down the thoughts of Ry for the second time that evening, refusing to let her emotions get the better of her. "Now go on. I have a duke to get ready for."

Rosina was almost certain that Lily wished to say more, but she released Rosina's hands and they both departed into their respective chambers.

Her lady's maid, Molly, was waiting for her once Rosina was on the other side of her chamber door.

"I assume you won't be alone this evening, my lady," Molly said, smirking at her and pulling out a sheer night rail.

Molly knew everything about her life, given that she had been with Rosina since she was a girl of five-and-ten. She was there when Rosina fell in love, when she married, and she was the one who held Rosina's hand and tried to force her to eat when she was devastated in the wake of her grief after Ry's passing. Molly had also been there the entire time since, encouraging Rosina to pick up the pieces of her life.

"You assume correctly," Rosina replied, turning so that Molly could unfasten the buttons of her dress.

"Please tell me it is that handsome duke I caught a glimpse of. The other maids were tittering about him."

Rosina laughed "It is, in fact, the very duke."

"As long as he treats you right, my lady," Molly said protectively. "Duke or not."

"I'm sure we shall pass a pleasant evening. He is surprisingly not as haughty and demanding as I might have expected. The title hasn't gone to his head yet."

Molly laughed. "Then you might still have time to tame him to be what you want." She pulled the dress over Rosina's head, then helped to remove her stays, chemise, and stockings. Rosina slipped the night rail over herself and then moved to the washbasin.

Rosina completed her evening ablutions while Molly tended to putting the worn garments away. After Rosina finished, Molly held out a purple satin robe for her and once she donned it, she tied it closed with the sash around her waist. Motioning for Rosina to sit at the mirror, Molly began brushing Rosina's hair as soon as she did so.

The pair chatted about some of the *on dit* from the servants that Molly had overheard, and who Rosina believed might pair up at the house party. With so many in close quarters and places to sneak off to, it was almost guaranteed that at least one couple would make such a declaration. It was a fun game to speculate about who the happy couple or couples might be.

Once Rosina's long blond hair was brushed, she had Molly leave it loose around her shoulders. Why bother putting it up when the handsome duke would just release it?

Molly departed after adding a couple more logs to the fire, and Rosina stared at herself in the mirror. Something nagged at her, but she wasn't certain what it was, or if she wished to explore it further. She had developed the practice of pushing such thoughts aside as a way of coping with the loss of Ry.

A knock sounded at her door. "Enter," she called out in a loud whisper.

Rosina stood from her seat and turned to see the duke sweep into her chamber, then close the door behind himself without so much as a sound other than the turn of the lock.

"So it would seem you didn't trick me," he said.

She took a few steps closer. "There are far more fun ways to toy with you, Duke."

Even in the low lighting from the candles and the roaring fire, she could see the tempting bulge forming between the duke's thighs. He certainly was quite reactive and easy to entice.

"You look beautiful, Lady Preston," he said, eyeing her from head to toe.

"Please call me Rosina, Duke. And I don't require pretty words, Your Grace. You needn't be afraid to dispense with such pretense and say what you wish in moments of passion. All I require from you is an orgasm and respect."

He choked on the night air. "I shall do my best to tend to both."

"And as for your own climax. You may spend in my mouth or my arse but never inside my cunt."

That time he choked harder, and it took him several coughs to recover. "What?"

"I know it should go without saying, but it's best to establish such rules up front. Given we have no desire to wed, we must do what we can to avoid an unexpected surprise."

He patted his chest, and after a few moments, seemed to have his coughing fit under control. She assumed he wasn't used to hearing a lady so boldly set the terms of such encounters, but she didn't wish to wait to have the conversation when his cock was inside of her.

"I quite agree." His words came out low and gravelly.

She took the remaining steps to close the distance between them and began working the buttons of his coat. "Very well, Your Grace. Where would you like to begin?"

He grabbed her wrist to halt her movements. "There is something else we must discuss first."

Rosina eyed him curiously. "Of course, please continue."

"I…uh…well…"

She wasn't certain she had ever heard a duke struggle to find his words and simply speak what was on his mind. Rosina nodded to him, urging him to continue. What could possibly be so difficult for him to say to her?

"It's just that I have never actually…been intimate with anyone." He closed his eyes, and she believed his face would be the color of a beet if he were illuminated by more than candlelight.

Rosina did her best to hide her shock, to not make him feel more embarrassed than he clearly already was about his admission. "Oh…well…" But she struggled to find her own words. Of anything he might have shared with her, she hadn't expected that.

"It should go without saying that I require your discretion in this matter."

She nodded. "Of course."

He ran his hands along his thighs. "I hoped you might tutor me."

"Tutor you?" She did her best to keep her face even, still in shock at what had been shared, and far too curious about how and why he had remained a virgin, when most men took to brothels and doxies as soon as they could.

"Yes." He sighed. "I want to experience everything and learn what to do for you."

Something about the idea of teaching him the art of coupling made her heart race and her thighs damp. He would be hers to mold and tame, at least for the duration of the house party. The duke expected her to tell him exactly what she wanted and how to give it to her, and the notion was thrilling.

Grinning at him, she licked her lips. "I shall be your willing tutor."

# Chapter 5

The tension in James' shoulders released as soon as she agreed to continue their arrangement. He wasn't certain what he would have done if she had sent him on his way, or worse, laughed or mocked him. His breeches were already stretched to their limit, and he could hardly wait for what they would do together.

"Have you ever seen a naked woman, Duke?"

He shook his head. "Only drawings and statues."

"Well, we should rectify that now. Should we not?" she asked, untying the sash that held her robe closed.

Clasping the sides of her robe, she held it closed. "Sit on the edge of the bed, Duke."

He finished removing the coat she had unbuttoned and then shucked his waistcoat and cravat and tossed them aside before sitting where she told him to.

"Go ahead and remove your boots, too," she commanded.

He rid himself of his boots and socks as quickly as he could and fixed his gaze on the perfect, beautiful woman before him. "Can I see you now?"

She moved so she stood before him, just out of reach. Opening the robe, she let each sleeve fall from her arms and the satin pooled around her feet when it hit the floor. James' breath caught at the sight of her form beneath the sheer material and the throb between his legs ached.

Reaching for his falls, he unfastened the first button.

"Not yet, Your Grace."

He groaned and moved his hands back to his sides. "Rosina…"

She bunched the fabric of her night rail at her sides and then pulled it over her head, leaving her naked before him. The sight of her left him speechless, a wave of intensity crashing over him. She was an ethereal goddess. Her blond hair kissed the globes of her full breasts, and her trim waist curved into hips he had the strongest urge to grip. His gaze settled on the nest of curls that hid the place he most desired to touch and explore.

His cock would surely finish the job he started if his buttons didn't hold out.

She stepped closer to him, positioning herself between his legs. "Touch me, Duke."

"Where?" he asked, desiring more than anything to feel the softness of her skin.

"Everywhere," she whispered.

He immediately raised both hands to cup her breasts. Her skin was just as soft as he knew it would be, and the flesh of her breasts molded to his hands. He massaged them, and she released a whimper when his thumb brushed over her nipple. The skin formed a tight, tempting bud. He brushed his thumb over it again, and a hard jolt shot to his cock when it elicited the same response.

James knew enough from hearing about his friends' conquests that mouths were used for far more than kissing, and unable to stop himself, he leaned forward and sucked her nipple into his mouth. Her hands shot to his head, and she arched her back with each of his sucks and licks.

"You are a quick study, Duke."

He shifted his head to give the same attention to her other breast, reveling in the faint taste of the floral notes on her skin. Without warning, she climbed on his lap and straddled him while he remained in an upright position.

"Is there anywhere else you might like to touch?" she asked.

Gripping her hips, he moved one hand to her front and brushed his fingers over the place between her legs. She let him explore on his own, and he shifted his fingers further inside her folds until the tips of his fingers were coated in wetness.

"You are damp there," he ground out.

"That means I like what you are doing to me, Duke." She placed her hand over his and urged his middle finger inside of her. His eyes rolled to the back of his head from imagining what his cock would feel like coated in the proof of her desire.

Rosina moved his hand again, urging him to withdraw his finger. She moved his hand further back and placed her finger on top of his middle finger as she pressed it against the tight hole of her arse. He watched her face, and she delighted in what they were doing. He wasn't certain which part of her intrigued him the most, but he wanted his fingers, tongue, and cock inside all of her.

Moving his hand again, she brought him to a nub at the opening to her slit. She guided him to circle his finger around it and rocked herself against his hand while she did so. "Various combinations of touching me in the places I showed you will bring me to orgasm," she said between pants.

She moved his hand away from her and returned to a standing position before him and began working the buttons of his shirt as she pressed her lips to his. James instantly parted his mouth to her and swept his tongue inside, taking control of their kiss. She may have given him his first kiss earlier that day, but he wouldn't be a passive bed partner. His goddess would know that he would be just as passionate of a lover after a bit of guidance.

Once she unfastened the last button, she pushed his shirt off his shoulders. She stood up straight and broke their kiss.

"Now, Duke," she commanded, "you may free your cock."

The word on her lips almost made him come unhinged. He fumbled with the buttons but finally revealed himself so his cock protruded proudly from his lap.

When she wrapped her hand around his shaft, he drew in a large breath of air and his head rolled back. Even just *her* hand instead of his was already the most exquisite thing he'd ever felt, and he knew it was only going to become more intense with each wicked thing she did to him.

"I love how responsive you are to my touch, Duke."

He responded with a low groan when she stroked his shaft again.

"Stand up and remove your breeches," she said, releasing him. He immediately hated the loss of her touch and lumbered to his feet and pushed his breeches to the floor.

Before he knew what was happening, she knelt before him on the floor. Looking down at her, she was by far the most beautiful woman he had ever seen. Her eyelids were heavy, and he knew she wasn't unaffected by him, and it took the edge off his inferior feelings regarding bed sport.

"I am going to lick and suck you until you come, Duke, and then I'm going to tutor you on how to do the same for me."

She licked the bottom of his shaft from the base to the tip, looking up at him as she did so, and the action alone was almost enough to make him spend.

"Fuck," he groaned. He certainly wouldn't last very long.

Rosina closed her lips around his cock and sucked so hard that he was certain he might totally lose his eyesight. She moved her mouth up and down his shaft, and he instinctively clasped her head in his hands.

He bit his bottom lip and rocked his hips into her mouth, meeting her sucks so she took him deeper into her mouth. She moaned and hummed against his cock, urging him on.

James increased the speed of his hips.

"Mm-hm," she mumbled with her mouth full of his member. She appeared to take pleasure from him using her mouth in that way, and it made him want to do so even more.

He continued moving himself deeper inside her mouth. "That's so fucking good."

Glancing down, he saw she had her hand between her legs, touching herself while she sucked him. He fucked her mouth harder, and his ballocks tightened just before he held her head still and released himself inside of her willing mouth.

The intensity of his climax had lasted more than several seconds and reached the tips of his fingers and toes. James stumbled back and dropped onto the bed, uncertain if his legs would continue to hold him. He reached for her and easily lifted her from the floor and into his lap.

He placed several kisses along the corner of her lips and then her jaw. "You didn't finish yourself, did you?" he growled against her ear.

"No, Your Grace." She gave him a coy grin, then gasped when he kissed and sucked along the line of her neck. The goddess had unleashed everything he'd been holding back since he'd become a man, and his primal instincts had taken over. He scooped her in his arms and stood so he could place her on her back on the bed.

Crawling on top of her, he kissed her again. His cock was already hard and ready again, pressed against her curls. "I'm going to taste the sweet honey between your legs, and then I'm going to fuck you."

"There's the foul-mouthed duke I hoped to meet," she said, grinning at him.

Unable to wait any longer, he licked and sucked his way down her body until his head was positioned between her legs on the bed. Spreading her thighs further apart, he lowered his tongue to meet the area that Rosina had him circle with his fingers. He knew he had found the right spot when she moved beneath him. Her hands flew to his head, and he relished the feel of her moving her hips against him to take her pleasure the way he had from her.

James shifted lower so he could stick his tongue inside of her, tasting where his cock would go. He moved his tongue, and she gripped his head tighter. In a moment of boldness, he shifted even lower and flicked his tongue against the puckered hole of her arse.

"You'll enjoy fucking me there," she panted.

He was inclined to agree with her. She would allow him to experience all of his fantasies before they departed from the party.

Running his tongue from her arse all the way back to the nub that made her buck and moan, he sucked the nub into his mouth.

Rosina held his head there. "Don't stop, Duke."

She undulated against his face and released the sweetest moans that made his cock twitch. Her breathing became ragged, and she bucked beneath him when she cried out, muffling herself with her hand.

Eager and ready to be inside her, he shifted so that he hovered over her again. Her breathing was still quick as her chest rose and fell beneath him. He might become addicted to the sight of her, sated after he brought her to climax, which was a crazy thought, and he instantly pushed it aside.

James positioned the head of his cock at her opening. He looked into her eyes to gauge if she wanted him to enter her. The goddess responded by wrapping her legs around his waist to hold him in place, and he pushed himself fully inside of her.

Freezing in place for only a moment, he took in the sensation of being sheathed inside of her. Her mouth had been delightful, but burying himself inside her tight cunt was another matter entirely. He thrust himself inside, taking her in long, deep strokes, experimenting with how to move his body and what she responded to.

"Duke," she moaned.

"James," he ground out. "When my cock is inside of you, I want to hear my name from your lips."

He thrust into her again, the confidence in his movements growing.

"James," she moaned again.

The sound of his name made him wild, and he fucked her with abandon. Her fingernails dug into his back, and he was almost certain they'd leave marks. Not that he cared. He'd proudly wear the marks of her branding him. She panted and moaned his name again as he felt her cunt clench and pulse around his cock.

He thrust again and remembered himself just in time so he pulled out of her, giving himself two more strokes with his hand before he shot several streams of his seed across her stomach.

James wanted nothing more than to collapse beside her, but he knew the gentlemanly thing to do would be to retrieve a cloth and clean her. He left the bed to do just that, grabbed a cloth from beside her washbasin, and dabbed it in the water. Walking back to the bed, he took in the sight of her lying across the bed, her chest heaving, eyes closed, with her hair splayed out beside her and splattered with his seed. She was breathtaking.

Something tugged at his insides, and he shrugged it off as he returned to her and wiped away the proof of what had occurred between them. She came up on her elbows and watched him.

"Was your first time everything you hoped it would be, Duke?"

Any response he gave would be an understatement. "It surpassed all my expectations, my lady. You are quite the tutor."

"Come back tomorrow, and I'll teach you a few more things."

There wasn't a single thing that would keep him from doing so. Now that he'd experienced the ecstasy of what it meant to be with a woman, he was certain his appetite wouldn't remain sated for very long.

Part of him longed to climb back on top of the beautiful woman before him and bury himself inside of her again, but Rosina had lain back and released a deep yawn. It had grown quite late already, and he should pace himself given that every night remaining in the house party awaited them.

He leaned over her and placed a light kiss on her lips. "I am eager to be under your tutelage. Among other things. Especially when the tutor is so beautiful."

She smirked at him and rolled her eyes. Rosina may believe his words to be hollow flattery, but everything he said was true. Even if there wasn't a future between them, there wasn't any harm in finding her irresistible.

He imagined it would only make the physical nature of their arrangement more satisfying.

James collected his clothing from around the room and dressed himself enough so that he could hurry to his own chamber. He started towards the door to depart.

"I shall see you at breakfast, my lady."

"Indeed, Your Grace."

He turned back to face her and leaned against the door.

"You should call me James when I'm not in your bed, too. In private, at least."

She grinned at him, and he ignored how his heart raced.

"Good night, James."

He gave her a small nod. "Good night, Rosina."

James unlocked the door and cracked it open so he could see if anyone was lurking in the hallway. Turning back to look at her one last time, he winked at her. "Minx."

# Chapter 6

The next morning, Rosina sat before the mirror while Molly styled her hair for the day. She had already donned her dark blue riding habit since there would be a riding party directly after breakfast. She didn't see the point in donning a morning dress for breakfast just to return to her chamber to change again.

"So? How was he?" Molly asked.

"Molly!" Rosina pretended to be scandalized, but she had spoken of such things with Molly for years. She could trust Molly with anything and everything.

Her maid laughed. "It's been so long since I've enjoyed a man. You can't blame me if I am a bit curious."

"He was quite passionate," Rosina said. "And indeed a satisfying experience. I believe he shall return this evening."

Molly clucked. "Of course he will." She swept more tresses of Rosina's hair back and placed a few pins.

Rosina wondered why the duke had been a virgin. He told her when they'd met that he came here for her. So his aim had been specifically for her to teach him. She had been far too ready to introduce him to pleasures of the flesh that she hadn't taken a moment to ask him why. Perhaps she never would.

Molly handed Rosina the riding bonnet that matched her habit. "I look forward to hearing more."

Rosina waved her off and departed her chamber. She made her way to the breakfast room. Even if she wouldn't admit it to herself, she was disappointed when she didn't see James in attendance yet. No, not James, she reminded herself. He was still the duke. Better to think on what would be an acceptable way to refer to the man in her thoughts instead of pondering why it grated on her nerves that he wasn't in the breakfast room.

She ventured to the sideboard and picked up a plate to make her selections.

"Good morning, Lady Preston," the very voice called from behind her as if Rosina had conjured him. "I do hope you slept well."

He joined her side and took a plate for himself. When she glanced over at him, he flashed her a knowing look at the shared secret between them. His presence caused an immediate reaction between her legs.

"I did, indeed, Your Grace." She scooped a portion of eggs onto her plate.

"I am glad to hear it." He leaned closer to where only she could hear. "You'll need your rest for tonight."

Her skin heated, and she stepped away from him to make a few more selections, hoping no one had noticed her reaction to him. She wasn't one to simper over a man, and yet she was flushed with a damp cunt from James. The duke, she corrected, again.

Rosina finished filling her plate and moved to take a seat at the table. After setting her plate down, she went to reach for her chair. The duke had beat her to it, pulling it out for her to sit. He placed his own plate down beside hers and took the seat to her right after she had settled into her chair.

"Are you going on the ride today?" he asked, spreading jam on a toast point.

"Indeed, I am. Will you also join?"

"I wouldn't miss the chance to be in the presence of a beautiful lady."

She rolled her eyes at him and then glanced at the other guests nearby to see if anyone paid attention to them. She noted that Miss Stone appeared displeased that the duke was paying Rosina attention instead of her.

"I believe there will be several on the ride, Your Grace."

"I shan't notice," the duke said.

Miss Stone would be further displeased, it would seem.

She jerked her head back towards him. "Your Grace," she whispered, warning him to keep his voice down.

He shrugged. "I have no intention of marrying, as you well know."

"You have brothers? Do you not?" she asked, changing the subject, since their conversation was sure to only stir up gossip if they should be overheard.

"I do."

The duke beamed, the same as if he were a proud father. And for some reason, her heart beat faster.

"Walter and William," he continued. "They are twelve."

"So they are at Eton, then?" She speared a piece of her fruit before bringing it to her mouth.

"Indeed." He beamed again, but she noted a flash of worry in his expression.

"Have you received an update on how they fare?"

He shook his head. "Not yet. I haven't received so much as a letter from the boys or their teachers."

The concern in his tone was evident, and her heart went out to him. It was obvious that his brothers were very dear to him. "I am sure they are well, Duke. You would have heard from the school if not."

"Of course," he reasoned. "You are right."

"I have my moments," she said, teasing him.

His brow relaxed, and he smirked at her. "That you do."

Shifting the conversation back to his brothers, since that was a far safer topic of conversation and might keep him from looking at her in ways that continued to make her thighs damp, she spoke again. "I assume you informed them of where to find you."

"I wrote to the school and to the boys before I departed and informed my household to ensure any correspondence was delivered to me immediately." His brow furrowed again, but he shook it off. "I know they will be all right. But I have cared for them since they were but seven years old."

Pain marred his expression for a fleeting moment before he schooled his features.

She opened her mouth to speak, to ask him about his parents, but Lord Duncan, a viscount who had been paying extra attention to Lady Juliet—not that she appeared to accept his suit—took the seat on the other side of His Grace and engaged him in conversation.

Rosina focused on her breakfast and ignored the gentlemen's conversation. She couldn't help but feel a strong sense of curiosity about what had happened to the duke's parents. The whole of society did not know the details about their deaths, and she only heard whispers indicating injuries of some kind. The duke appeared to harbor a lot of responsibility for his brothers, which was admirable. It left her wondering why he didn't wish to wed.

She pushed aside the thoughts and questions. It was of no matter to her why he didn't wish to wed. He had his reasons, and they were of no import to her. She only wanted him for the pleasure they could experience together, and the rest of it was his business.

Once breakfast was finished, she made her way out to the stables with the duke fast on her heels. She knew he was behind her since his intoxicating scent of sandalwood was just as strong as it had been from where he sat beside her at the table.

Not glancing back, she continued on her way until she was outside. He fell into step beside her as they approached the stables. Once they arrived, a groom set off to saddle a horse for each of them and Rosina placed her riding bonnet on her head and secured the sash beneath her chin.

The groom positioned her horse by the mounting block, but the duke gripped her hips and lifted her into the saddle. When he removed his hands from her, she instantly felt the loss of his touch. She caught his gaze where he stood below her, her chest rising and falling as their eyes held.

The sound of other guests approaching reminded her of where she was, and she grabbed the reins and better positioned herself in the saddle. The duke mounted the horse beside her, and they sat in silence as if neither were quite sure what to say to each other.

A quarter hour later, the rest of the guests had joined and had all mounted their horses for the riding party. Their hosts led the way, and the group paired off in smaller groups, following behind. She half expected the duke to trot off and seek the company of a gentleman in attendance, but he trotted beside her, their horses falling into the same pace.

She glanced at the other guests and noted that Miss Stone had paired off with Lord Percy. She spoke up at him through her lashes and seemed to have decided that her efforts would be futile with the duke. Something about that realization made Rosina grin.

"Should you be seen spending so much time with me, Duke? I am quite scandalous, if you didn't know." Her tone was one of jest, but it was true that he had already spent a lot of time in her company.

"It's one of my favorite qualities about you," he teased. He glanced over his shoulder and then continued. "Besides, I am a duke. I shall threaten anyone who wags their tongue with the cut direct."

She gave him a sideways glance. "I wondered how long it would take for you to embrace your role as the not-to-be-crossed duke."

"Might as well use it to my advantage." The mirth in his tone had returned, which was in stark contrast to the threat the man had just made.

They rode together in silence for several moments. Rosina noticed the clouds in the sky, and that one looked almost like an elephant. She laughed to herself and then a wave of emotion washed over her and tears formed at the corners of her eyes. Trying to avoid the duke seeing her, she glanced away and attempted to wipe her eyes.

"Is something the matter?"

No such luck.

"It's nothing." Her voice caught on the last syllable as much as she tried to fight it. She drew a deep breath and regained control of herself.

"Rosina," he said, his tone softer than she'd ever heard him. The tenderness threatened the hold she had on her memories and her tears.

She shook her head and focused her gaze forward.

"Something has upset you. Please tell me what it is. Just because our arrangement is one of a physical nature doesn't mean we can't speak as friends."

"It's nothing you wish to hear, Your Grace."

"Allow me to be the judge of that," he urged.

She sighed a deep exhale. "See that cloud just there?" she asked, pointing to the sky.

He glanced in the direction where she pointed. "The one that looks like an elephant?"

Her heart panged, and she swallowed hard. "My husband used to see shapes in all the clouds. He'd point them out to me when we rode together. Sometimes I swore he just made up something ridiculous, and other ones, like that one there, were more obvious."

The duke said nothing, and she glanced over at him. He was still watching the sky.

"I'm sorry, Your Grace," she said. "But I did warn you."

"You have nothing to apologize for, Rosina."

Her body tensed at how he used her given name again. They continued on in silence, and she wondered if he would change his mind about riding alongside her. When the party reached another open field, they took off into a gallop together and raced across the grass. The wind against her face helped to settle her nerves, and the tension in her shoulders eased.

They reached an area where several picnic locations had been set up. There were five large blankets with a basket in the middle of each one that contained their repast. Before she could climb down from her horse, the duke was in front of her, lifting her down.

Her skin heated beneath where his gloved hands gripped her body. Guilt washed over her as the only other man she had such a reaction to had been Ry. It had to be because Ry had been in her thoughts. The duke was handsome, to be sure, and a quick study in the art of pleasure, but it was nothing more than that. Her body was all too aware of the pleasure he could give her, and that was all it was. It was all it could be.

After the awkward conversation about Ry, Rosina thought it best to join one of the blankets where other guests were present. It would help dissuade talk as well if they didn't sit alone. Lady Eliza sat on the first blanket with Lord Irvine, so Rosina urged the duke there and took a seat on the blanket near Lady Eliza.

The four of them passed a pleasant time enjoying the chicken and cheese that had been prepared, along with lemonade and a bit of wine. The gentlemen spoke of horses and places Lord Irvine thought the duke ought to visit soon, while Rosina chatted with Eliza about each of their plans when they returned home from the house party.

Rosina had the impression that Irvine had intentions for the beautiful Lady Eliza, but she didn't believe the lady shared his affections. She seemed a bit distracted and didn't act the part of the woman who hoped that a man might court her.

Rosina believed that to be the best based on what she knew of Irvine. He didn't have the best reputation, and his intentions were likely to be something untoward.

Catching the duke's eye, it sent shockwaves through her body, and she fought a tremble. Something about him drew her to him like a child to the window of a sweets shop. He was the perfect confection and as much as she tried to push thoughts of him aside, she wanted more.

A thick blanket of dark clouds was rolling in, and the gentlemen helped the ladies to their feet, then they all hurried to their horses. James lifted her up, doing nothing to ease the ripples of electricity that coursed through her.

"I think we are going to need to make haste, my lady."

"I should think so," she said, glancing up at the sky.

They trotted off, the first of the group to depart back to the Ockhams' stables.

"I am sorry if I upset you earlier," the duke said.

She flinched, not intending to make him feel poorly over the memory she had of Ry. "It is the way of a widow, Your Grace. Sometimes the memories can't be helped. There are times when the pain is unbearable, and then there are moments when the pain has subsided. The longer that Ry has been gone, the more days I have where the pain is far more tolerable." Rosina wasn't sure why she told him all of that and regretted it the moment the words escaped her lips.

"You were a love match."

It wasn't a question. He was acknowledging as much from her words and from the way her voice had caught when she spoke. "Yes."

"My parents were a love match," he said. Even only glancing at his profile, she could see the sadness marring his expression. "My father grieved for my mother every day until he passed. He would forget that she had done so, and I had to break his heart all over again when he turned frantic, wanting to go to her."

"James," she whispered before she could think better at using his given name. "I'm so sorry. That must have been awful for you to watch."

His chin jerked in her direction. "I'm sorry you lost your husband."

The intensity of his gaze and his heartfelt, caring tone heated her skin. Which made her angry at herself for betraying Ry's memory. She just spoke of her love for Ry, and then every part of her body wanted the man beside her.

There was a crack of lightning, surrounded by an enormous crash of thunder. Rosina shook off her confused reaction. "We must gallop."

James snapped his head forward, and they both urged their horses to gallop across the field. They raced through the grass and were the first of the guests to reach the stables, only catching a few drops before they were safely within the building. The rain came down in buckets just after the duke had lifted her down from her horse.

The groom handed them an umbrella, and the duke opened it so they could share. He urged her forward and wrapped his arm around her as they hurried across the grass to enter the house as a group of other guests arrived, having been soaked from getting caught in the rain. The feeling of him so close and the scent of sandalwood she would forever associate with him stirred what had been boiling within her.

When they reached the entrance to the house, the duke folded the umbrella and leaned it in the corner near the doorway. She noticed the way his thighs flexed beneath his skin-tight breeches when he leaned over to do so. She was no better than a bitch in heat.

She grabbed his hand and pulled him with her.

"Rosina…er, Lady Preston?"

"Come with me," she said.

He didn't protest and allowed her to pull him down the long corridor until they reached the foyer that led to the grand staircase. The other guests would emerge soon, seeking their chambers to change into dry clothes, so they must hurry.

After pulling him up the stairs and to her chamber, she opened her door and dragged him inside.

"My lady," Molly said, shocked as she worked on what Rosina expected would be the dress Molly had selected for her to wear to dinner.

"Molly, will you return in an hour?"

Her faithful maid smirked at her and carefully put the dress to the side. "Of course, my lady." She nodded to James. "Your Grace."

As soon as Molly departed and closed the door behind her, Rosina locked it, then threw herself against the duke, practically climbing him like a cat climbed a tree to catch its prey. She took his lips, and when he wrapped his arms around her, she gripped his cravat and jerked it loose from his neck.

Their tongues warred with an unbridled frenzy as she worked the buttons of his coats and his shirt beneath until all hung open, but still on his shoulders, giving her access to rub her hands across his chest into the smattering of dark hair.

He groaned and grabbed her wrists.

"Rosina."

"Remove your clothing, Duke."

He didn't release her wrists or do as she instructed, so she pulled back so she could look at him. The duke watched her as if he were searching for something in her expression.

"Our arrangement isn't one of affection and attachment, and I am truly sympathetic to your loss, but I don't wish to be with a woman while she thinks about another man."

"Duke, I am not—"

"You don't think," he started, cutting her off. "I noticed how you were lost in thought and in a state of unease. And then you bring me to your bed?"

She closed her eyes and drew a breath, trying to find the words to convince him of how wrong he was. "James," she whispered. "I have been in a state of unease because my body wants you. You. That confuses and hurts my heart to acknowledge so, but I assure you that right now, I am wet with anticipation from thinking of you."

He released a low growl and pulled her wrists so that her body was against his, then took her lips again. James released her wrists, and she spun around so he could aid in removing her riding habit. Once he released each of the buttons, he lifted the dress over her head, bringing her chemise with it. She had never been more thankful that she wasn't wearing stays.

Rosina turned to face him, and he was shrugging out of his already unbuttoned coats and shirts. She leaned down to remove her stockings.

"Stop," he commanded, staring at her otherwise naked form. The wetness reached her thighs from the way he ran his tongue along his bottom lip. He unbuttoned his breeches and pushed them down around his hips. "Leave them on."

# Chapter 7

As much as it would have killed him, James had been ready to walk away from her. He might have wanted to dip his wick in the luscious woman before him more than anything in the world, but he had a bit too much pride to do so if he thought she would just close her eyes and pretend he was another man. He wasn't sure why such a notion bothered him so much, since their arrangement was one of enjoying each other for pleasure, yet it irked him.

Thankfully, he hadn't needed to test his resolve after her declaration. His cock ached at the sight of her. While he kicked off his hessian boots so he could free his legs from his breeches, she grabbed something from her dresser drawer. He couldn't help but notice how her arse rounded, and he moved close and cupped both cheeks with his hands, squeezing the soft flesh.

She sighed and leaned back against him, and he slipped one of his hands deeper between her legs, drawing a deep breath when his fingers were met with the wet heat of her folds.

Rosina spun around and pushed against him, walking him backwards until the back of his bare legs were against the settee. She urged him to sit and then straddled him, allowing his shaft to rub against her.

Cupping her breasts so he could massage them, he kissed along her shoulder and neck until he reached her lips. She sucked his tongue into her mouth and raised herself off his lap and then lowered so she speared herself with his cock.

"Bloody hell," he whispered against her lips when she took all of him in the single movement.

She pressed her hands against his chest and pushed him against the back of the settee while she rocked herself against him.

"Do not come, James," she commanded, throwing her head back.

"I make no promises if you keep taking me like this."

She rocked against him a few more times and then lifted herself off him, still straddling him with his cock protruding between them.

"Why on earth did you stop?" he ground out.

"Because if you wish to come inside me, you must insert yourself somewhere else," she said, beautiful mischief written all over her features.

His cock twitched, and he wasn't certain he could possibly be any harder.

She reached for a jar he had long forgotten that she'd sat on the cushion beside them, opened it, and held it up to him. "Coat your fingers."

Willing to do whatever she directed, he did so and realized it was oil. His heart beat faster when he realized what she intended and shifted his hand beneath her. He slowly rubbed the oil around the tight opening of her arse. "Stick your finger inside," she panted.

Needing no further invitation, he slid his index finger inside slowly, his eyelids heavy from the sensation of the tight hole around his finger. James added a second finger, coating the inside of her with the oil. She moved herself against his fingers, releasing the most enticing low stream of moans.

Before he knew what was happening, she must have dipped her own fingers in the oil, because she began coating his entire length with it. The sensation of her oiled hand moving up and down his shaft would have made him spend if she did so for very long.

She tugged at his arm to withdraw his fingers and then hovered herself over him, using her hand to guide the tip of his cock where she wanted him to be. Lowering herself slowly, she took more of him into her arse, and each movement was more exquisite than the last. When she fully seated herself with his entire length inside of her, he let his head fall over the back of the settee.

The siren moved, and he raised his head again to watch her. She slipped her hand to her nub while she moved herself on his cock. "Let me," he whispered, replacing her fingers with his. She panted and moaned while she rode him with her arse.

Her eyes drifted close, and he released a low growl. "Look at me," he ground out. "Don't take your eyes off mine."

Rosina's eyes blinked open, and she did as he said. He slipped two fingers into her cunt and used his thumb to tease the sensitive pearl, and her breath became even more ragged while she moved against him. "James," she moaned.

"Yes," he whispered. "Come on my fingers, and then I'm going to take you from behind." He knew enough from his friends' bar room talk to know that there were many positions. The closer she drew to her climax, something came unhinged in him. He needed to possess her.

To ensure there was no possible way she would think of another.

Her cunt clenched around his fingers, and she didn't remove her eyes from his when she shook and moaned his name over and over a few times. If he didn't know better, he might have thought that a part of his soul had become intertwined with hers from the intensity of the moment.

Taking her with him, he stood, withdrawing himself from inside her before he carried her to the bed, positioning her on her stomach. She hadn't yet caught her breath and lay flat on the coverlet. Crawling onto the bed, he hovered over her backside, placing a few kisses along her shoulder, then sucking her neck. Her skin was salty from her exertions, and he sucked her neck harder, not caring if he left a mark. He wanted to mark her. Some symbol to remind them both that he had been the one to do so.

She whimpered and panted. He allowed his cock to rest on her arse cheeks as he continued sucking and licking along her neck until he reached her ear. Her moans served as his indication that she liked what he was doing, given he still wasn't overly confident in his abilities. His primal instincts had long taken over and he just needed to touch and taste all of her most tempting places.

"Do you want me inside you?" he whispered into her ear.

She nodded, causing him to smile against her ear.

"You must tell me what to do, my beautiful tutor," he said, licking the soft, tender place just behind her ear.

When she moaned, he grinned again. He was a good student, indeed.

"James." She sighed. His cock stiffened even more at the use of his name.

"Yes?" He ran one of his hands slowly down her side, grazing his fingers over her soft skin until he reached her hip. Wedging his hand between her core and the bed, he used his fingers to tease her slit. "You didn't answer me."

"I want you," she finally said between pants and moans.

That was the response he hoped for. James shifted back on his knees between her legs. She shifted so her knees were beneath her, elevating her bottom to give him better access. He massaged the exposed area of her thighs that her stockings didn't cover, then spread her rounded cheeks apart and with painful slowness slid his cock back inside of the tight hole of her arse.

Enjoying the control of the position they were in, he knew he wouldn't last long after the first thrust. He gripped her hip with one hand and slid the other around her front to rub her pearl while he moved inside of her again.

"James," she moaned again. "That feels so good."

Part of him longed to puff his chest out with pride at her words, given his lack of experience, but instead, he thrust harder and faster inside of her. Increasing the speed with his hand, she bucked when she came again, moaning his name several times. He wasn't certain he would ever get enough of hearing her do so—and knowing he had been the one to make her react thus.

He turned feral, gripping her hips with both hands. He fucked her hard and fast for several thrusts before he pushed himself all the way to the hilt. Releasing deep inside of her, he filled her with every shot of his seed. In a territorial urge, he leaned over her and lightly bit into her neck, then smoothed the areas with his tongue.

James refused to ponder why he had such an intense reaction to her. Or why he needed her to want him so badly. He couldn't mistake a physical attraction for something more, and he wouldn't. He knew better and knew it wasn't anything more than enjoying the first woman he had ever been with in that way.

Withdrawing from her carefully, he shifted his feet to the floor so that he could collect a cloth to clean her. After doing so, she turned on her side and caught his gaze. They stared at each other for a few seconds, and he thought she might ask him something, but the question in her eyes disappeared as quickly as he saw it.

His throat tightened, and he had to remove himself from her presence. He longed to crawl into the bed and hold her, something he had never done with anyone before, and the mere idea of doing so scared him.

"I must dress before your maid returns." He began collecting his clothing and dressing himself.

Rosina had climbed down from the other side of the bed and covered herself with a robe, while James continued dressing himself. For James, the silence was palpable, and he reminded himself that he was being a fool. She was a beautiful woman, who was pleasing in bed. It was just a bonus that he also enjoyed spending time in her presence and conversing with her. He was reading too much into the intensity of the moment they had shared.

There was a knock at the door and Rosina shifted to confirm it was her maid. Once she had done so, she unlocked the door and let the woman slide into the room before closing the door again. James had already donned all his clothing and had just finished putting on his boots.

The woman smirked at James when she entered the room.

"Might you confirm if there is anyone in the hallway for me?" he asked of Rosina's maid.

"Of course, Your Grace." She poked her head back outside, then waved him to her. "It's clear. You must hurry."

Rosina stopped him. "Will you come here again tonight?"

"Indeed," he said as there was no question that he would do so. He wasn't certain he would be able to even wait until everyone went to bed to be with her again, and such a revelation would be problematic if he allowed himself to ponder it any further. "I'll see you at dinner."

Her maid stepped back so he could depart from Rosina's chamber and hurry down the hall before anyone could see where he came from.

The next morning, James blinked his eyes open when his valet entered the room and began readying James' clothing. He turned on his side, hiding his erection and willing it to subside, wondering how he could possibly be in such a state after the night he had spent with his goddess. They had coupled for hours, experimenting with a variety of positions.

But he must remember that she was not his. He didn't even wish to marry.

Well, that wasn't exactly true. He didn't wish to disrupt his brothers after all the pain their family had been through. Although seeing the pain his father went through made him question if he even wanted a love match.

He had spent the entire dinner and time afterwards in her presence talking and laughing when they hoped the rest of the party didn't notice. He found he just enjoyed having her near. He might be willing to admit that he felt just a bit more for the lady than he ought, but there was still the matter of the boys and the stability they needed.

Once he had dressed that morning, he joined the rest of the party for breakfast, taking an open seat next to Rosina. She had agreed to accompany him on the trip to town, and he was looking forward to enjoying her company just as much as he enjoyed what they did in her chamber. But it didn't mean anything, just that she was far more than a beautiful face who was good at bedsport. He could enjoy conversation with a woman and not have it mean anything more than that.

After they broke their fast, they joined the other guests in front of the house and waited for their carriage to transport them. There wasn't a cloud in the sky, so it was sure to be a pleasant day strolling through the shops and outdoor carts in the village.

"Is there something particular you like to shop for, Your Grace?" she asked.

"Perhaps something for my brothers." He wondered again how they were enjoying school.

She looped her arm in his. "You still have heard nothing from them?" The softness in her tone warmed his heart.

"Not yet. I keep hoping I'll receive a bundle of correspondence here." That was an understatement.

"I am sure you will hear something soon, and that all is well, Your Grace." She patted his arm, and her touch aided in reassuring him.

He drew a breath, tamping down his reaction to her. It wouldn't serve either of them well.

"Thank you, my lady."

She opened her mouth to speak but closed it again when Lord Demming approached.

"I thought you weren't feeling well, my lord," Rosina said, eyeing the man curiously. At breakfast, he had indicated he was suffering from a megrim.

He waved them off, but for a moment, he appeared almost as if something were troubling him. "I lay down for a few moments and then found I was feeling much better. I would enjoy a trip to the village, and I hope you don't mind if I join your carriage. I don't wish to give any of the eligible young misses the wrong idea."

James would have much rather had Rosina to himself in the carriage, but there was no path forward other than to agree, so he nodded to Demming.

"Spending time in my company might give them a different kind of idea," Rosina jested.

Demming gave her a small grin. "You don't expect me to believe you are truly as scandalous as all that, do you, my lady?"

Rosina shrugged. "I don't much care what anyone else should believe, my lord. I live for myself, not the feather-brained members of society."

Demming and James both laughed as a carriage stopped in front of them. James handed Rosina into the carriage. Before he could climb in for himself, Demming whispered, "I wish you luck in your endeavor, Your Grace."

"Whatever do you mean?"

"I know all too well what a besotted man looks like."

James clenched his jaw, trying to hide his annoyance. "I believe you are mistaken." Although James wasn't completely certain it was a mistake. He had become far more infatuated with the lady than he had ever intended.

He climbed into the carriage, not interested in giving Demming a chance to offer a retort. Even though he knew that taking the seat beside Rosina would earn him a knowing look from Demming, he did so anyway. The idea of Demming sitting next to her, their sides touching, irritated him, and the two broad-shouldered gentlemen sitting together would prove quite uncomfortable.

Just as he suspected, as soon as Demming took his seat, the man caught his eye and arched his brows before he shifted to stare out the carriage window.

They rode in silence for a few minutes and James noticed nothing except for how Rosina felt pressed against him. He had the strongest urge to put his arm around her and had to clasp his hands in his lap to keep from doing so. That would only give Demming even more cause to believe he was correct in his declarations.

Demming broke the silence. "I don't believe I ever got to offer you condolences for your parents, Your Grace."

"Thank you, my lord." James' tone wasn't one to encourage further words on the subject as he didn't prefer to speak about his parents.

Rosina glanced up at James and he noted the sympathy in her expression. She gave him a soft smile, and his heart did a flip in his chest.

"Your father was a good man," Demming continued. "He was quite proud of all his sons."

James swallowed the emotion that arose from the man's words. His throat was thick as he hoped his father would be proud of him. Proud that he had devoted his time and attention to caring for his brothers. Although his father would want him to marry and carry on the family line as he was expected to do and not pass the responsibility to one of those very same brothers.

Perhaps considering marriage wasn't the worst idea if he did so with the right woman. The woman must love his brothers, and they must love her. It was the only way it might work.

"We miss him very much," James finally spoke. "And our mother."

A few moments later, the carriage came to a stop at the beginning of the street in the village. James released a sigh of relief that he wouldn't have to discuss his parents any longer.

He stepped out of the carriage and then lifted Rosina down instead of offering her his hand. When Demming descended the carriage step. "I believe I shall go this way. I will see you both later."

Demming gave James a small nod, and he knew the man was intending to leave the pair alone on purpose. James wasn't sure if he was annoyed or thankful for the man doing so. He decided it was the latter as he wished to enjoy Rosina's company without the necessary pretense if others were to remain in their presence.

Rosina placed her hand in the crook of his arm and pulled him to stroll down the road in the opposite route that most of the other guests took.

"What happened to your parents?" she asked quietly where only he might hear.

So much for avoiding more conversation about them. He drew a deep breath. "They were attacked by highwaymen returning home from our London townhome."

She gasped. "I thought they were ill for an extended period."

James closed his eyes to steady himself. "They were injured in the attack. The complications of their injuries left them mostly bedridden and in a precarious condition. My mother passed almost a year after the attack, and then my father passed another two years after she did." She gripped his arm tighter, and it soothed him, making him wish she could wrap her slender arms around him.

"That must have been so awful for you and your brothers. Were you away at university while they were cared for at home?"

He shook his head. "I never attended university. My brothers didn't handle the ordeal very well. They were only seven when the attack happened." He glanced at her and she just stared back at him, remaining quiet so he might explain what he meant. "You see, my parents weren't like others of the ton. They were a love match and spent a lot of time with us. Before my brothers were born, well, and afterwards, my parents doted on me. They read me stories, took meals with me, Papa playcd with me on the floor, and they spent little time away from our country home. They were much the same with my brothers. We were a happy, contented family."

"That sounds like a wonderful life." They strolled through an outdoor market, mostly pretending to look at the wares.

"Indeed, it was." He sighed. "But after their attack, I had just returned from Eton. My mother was hardly awake and when she was, she experienced a lot of pain. I had her placed in the same room with my father since they didn't wish to be apart. Papa was a bit more himself but didn't quite have all of his faculties from the medications.

"The boys began having nightmares and soiled their beds in the night," he continued. "They acted out for their nanny during the day, and they weren't eating properly." James wasn't sure why he shared as much as he had. He never spoke of his parents or what his family went through.

Rosina had gasped a few times as he spoke. "Those poor boys," she said. "And you."

She glanced up at him, and the tenderness in her expression almost undid him. He always had to be his own pillar of strength for the last five years to ensure that his brothers endured, and the lady beside him was taking down the wall he had built around himself, brick by brick.

"It wasn't easy," he said, placing his free gloved hand on top of hers. He just needed to touch her. "I didn't attend university as planned and stayed with them. I read to them at night before bed as my parents did, and I helped with their lessons. We ate our meals together, just the three of us, and then we'd sit with our parents each afternoon. I had the boys read to them while they slept so they could practice doing so and to make it less scary for them to see Mama and Papa that way."

"You are a good man, and brother, Duke," she said, discreetly wiping her eyes. "It's no wonder you are so concerned for them while they are away."

"They have been as happy as could be expected, but being away at school is quite the adjustment."

She squeezed his arm tighter. "You have prepared them well. Far better than most brothers would."

"I will ensure they both attend university as I never did. Although, I suppose I have fared all right. My estates have prospered since I took up handling all our family business matters at eight-and-ten."

"Ry didn't attend university either," she said, glancing down at her feet as they continued strolling through another market. James wasn't certain he had glanced at a single costermonger since he had been so focused on their conversation.

"Why not?" James asked.

She drew a deep breath and released it. "Because we didn't wish to wait to marry. He was nine-and-ten, and I was a year younger."

James patted her hand, finding that he wished to know more about the man Rosina had loved. He found he wanted to know everything about her and her past. In that moment, he was almost certain that even though they had agreed that things between them would never progress beyond physical attraction, he felt something deeper for her. Without a hint of jealousy in his tone because there wasn't any, only a desire to know and understand her better, he asked, "Will you tell me about him?"

# Chapter 8

Rosina gasped at James' question. He seemed genuinely interested in knowing about Ry, even though she rarely spoke of him in that way to others. But after all he had shared with her and the pain he had endured from grieving his parents and supporting his brothers, she wanted to share that part of herself with him, even if she wasn't certain she should.

"What do you wish to know?"

"How did you meet?" He glanced at her for a moment before they turned a corner to walk down another street.

"Ry, Ryan, was my older brother's best friend. He lived a couple of estates away from us and I used to tag along with them everywhere they went. I was the annoying girl who wouldn't leave them alone, and then we became much more to each other."

"He must have loved you very much to forgo university and marry you so young."

She smiled, recalling the memory of the first time Ry had told her he loved her. "He did. We were…intimate before our marriage and had always intended to wed." She jerked her chin towards James, worried she might have overshared and would see a sour expression on his face, but all she saw was contemplation. It did something to her insides, and she did her best to control her breathing.

"What happened to him?" James asked softly.

"He developed an illness that made him quite sick. It started out with fainting spells, nausea, and pain in his stomach. It progressed over several months until he succumbed to the illness. The doctors said there was no cure for what he had." It was the first time she had spoken of Ry's illness without bursting into tears. After hearing what James went through with his parents, she believed if anyone might understand the pain of watching someone you love slip away right in front of you, it was him.

James turned his chin to catch her gaze. "I'm very sorry you lost him, Rosina."

Tears formed at the corners of her eyes from the sincerity in his tone. There was much more to the man at her side than she had realized before. He'd had her in every position imaginable, speaking wicked words the night before, and then could genuinely offer remorse for her losing her first love. No. Just her love. *First* would indicate she might have another.

"Thank you, James," she whispered, hoping no one was near enough to hear her refer to a duke by his given name. "I'm sorry you lost your parents and all you had planned for your future."

"I can't dwell on the past. I can only think about the future and be the man my brothers need me to be to guide them."

She thought about how they came to be in each other's sphere and how the duke had been a virgin before he pursued her.

"Is that why you never…before we…?" she asked, her voice trailing off.

He nodded. "I have been present for my brothers every day until they left for school. I was there for every meal and every report from their tutors. I worked with our estate managers and cared for my brothers. Once the incident occurred, I knew I must set an example for them," he said before glancing at her again and smirking. "At least for as long as I could."

"I don't believe your brothers shall be made aware of your lost virtue, Your Grace," she teased. "At least not from me."

"Who knows what mischievous things they have learnt from the other boys at school," he said, releasing a deep sigh. "I just wish I might hear something soon."

"You will make an amazing father one day," she said, but then regretted it as soon as she said it. Why was she thinking of the man as a father? The thought of him settling down and marrying another faceless lady gnawed at her more than she cared to admit.

He stopped and faced her. "Do you think I might make a passable husband one day as well?"

Yes, very much. "I suppose your wife shall be satisfied, Your Grace," she teased him. The woman he married would be more than satisfied, indeed, and she didn't care to imagine such an ending, since it would never be her. She didn't even wish for it to be her. Rosina knew she had already given her heart to Ry, and she couldn't stomach the idea of giving her heart another or again going through the pain she had with Ry.

James stared at her, tilting his head so that he gazed at her lips. "That's good to know, my lady," he whispered.

As much as her mind told her to back away, her body betrayed her and swayed closer to him. Licking her bottom lip, she tilted her chin up, pushing aside the thoughts of warning that told her to back away.

A carriage passed by, and Rosina quickly stepped back, remembering they were standing in the middle of a village street. It wouldn't do for anyone to have caught them as they were. It was one thing to suspect they may have an arrangement. It was another matter entirely if anyone were to witness and confirm the notion.

"I should like to look at the quills at the stand, Your Grace," she said, not meeting his eye and urging them to continue walking.

The rest of their time in the village was spent engaging in light conversation. Rosina kept them closer to other guests from the party so they might not be tempted to act in such a brazen manner again. The duke selected a couple of gifts for his brothers while they explored more of the shops, seemingly forgetting what had almost occurred between them.

After dinner that evening, Rosina mingled with some of the other guests. She had spent so much time in the duke's presence that it was better for both of them to be seen interacting with others. At least that was what she told herself. Even if she spoke with others, her body was acutely aware of his presence at all times.

Each time he laughed or she heard his voice, she glanced over to see who he was speaking with. Once, when she caught his gaze, he winked at her, and her heart flipped. She wouldn't have been bothered if her skin merely heated or she had to clinch her thighs together at the sight of him, which she also did, but the way his presence touched her heart was another matter of concern.

Rosina did her best to pay attention during the game of charades until she could politely retire for the evening. Once she was in her chamber, Molly helped to ready her for bed. Or at least for activities that might or might not take place in a bed.

"Something troubling you, my lady?" Molly asked, brushing Rosina's hair.

"It's nothing," Rosina replied, a bit more clipped than she should have.

"I believe we both know that isn't true," Molly replied, biting back a bit of annoyance. "Is it His Grace? Did he do something to offend you, my lady?" The concern was evident in her tone.

Rosina shook her head, and Molly placed her head back in the position she wanted it in to continue brushing.

"He has done nothing wrong," Rosina said, her words almost a sigh.

Molly watched her in the mirror from where she stood behind Rosina, no longer brushing her hair. Tilting her head, she assessed Rosina. Her eyes widening, Molly gasped. "You have feelings for him."

"Of course not."

"Hmmm." Molly resumed brushing Rosina's hair.

Molly's reaction frustrated Rosina to no end. "And what is that supposed to mean?" she asked, not bothering to hide her annoyance.

"Nothing at all," Molly said, waving her off. "Do you wish for your hair to be fixed in a plait or left down?"

"Leave it down." She was certain that Molly hadn't said all that she truly thought, but Rosina also wasn't certain she wished to hear her maid's opinions. She knew her own mind. At least she believed she did. She certainly had before she arrived at the dratted house party.

Molly departed and left Rosina alone as she waited for James. She wasn't certain how long it would be before he arrived, given that many of the guests were still awake and moving about the house.

She lay across her bed, resting her head on her pillow and staring at the canopy that covered the bed. She didn't have feelings for the duke. Molly was mistaken.

Closing her eyes, she recalled Ry's face and the way he would grin at her. Slowly, his face morphed into James', and she fought to make the image return to her Ry's. Tears fell down her cheeks, and she grabbed a pillow to hug against her. Softly crying, she drifted off to sleep.

Lying in her bed, the morning sky was light outside the window as dawn approached. Rosina turned to face away from the window and there was something heavy across her waist. The scent of sandalwood overwhelmed her senses. James. She blinked her eyes open, and the very man was beside her, asleep in her bed with his arm draped over her.

Somehow, he was even more handsome with his face relaxed in a state of deep sleep. When had he entered her chamber? She was still in her night rail and robe, while he had removed his coats and shirt but donned his breeches.

Unable to resist, she ran her hand along his chest, then pushed back the hair that had fallen across his forehead.

He blinked open his eyes and just grinned at her.

"What are you doing here?" she asked.

"I came to see you and you looked too peaceful to awaken."

She sighed. "But what are you doing here? Why were you asleep in my bed?"

"I wished to hold you while you slept," he said as if it were the most reasonable thing in the world. "I have never done so with anyone."

She wouldn't allow herself to admit that it felt good to be in his arms that way, or that she had slept more peacefully than she had in a long time.

Before she could attempt to protest, he leaned forward and placed a tender kiss on her lips. She closed her eyes, the electricity from his lips overtaking her senses. He deepened the kiss, and she leaned into him, sweeping her tongue into his mouth. She kissed him with fervent need until something nagged at her and caused her to pull back.

"This isn't part of our arrangement," she said with a breathy tone as she fought to regain control over herself.

"But it could be. Do you mean to tell me you don't sense what has been growing between us?"

She sensed it, but she didn't wish to admit it. "James," she whispered, a pained edge to her tone.

"Rose, please," he said.

Her eyes flung open, and she scrambled from the bed. "Never call me that," she ground out, wrapping her arms around herself. As much as she willed them away, tears streamed down her cheeks.

"I'm sorry," he said. "I didn't mean…I don't understand…"

"Just go," she said, giving him her back. "Go now." Her shoulders shook as she fought the sobs.

"Rosina," he said from behind her. "I care about you. I know I promised I wouldn't—"

She couldn't hear anymore. "Please leave. I don't wish to speak to you."

"But—" he started before she cut him off.

"Your Grace, I have asked you to leave." Her words came out between sobs. She couldn't bear to face him or see what reaction he had to her outburst. Her shoulders shook, and she fought to calm herself.

She heard the fumbling of clothing, and several moments later, the door opened and closed. Rosina glanced over her shoulder to confirm he had left and then threw herself on the bed, muffling her guttural sobs into her pillow.

Allowing herself to have feelings for James, let alone loving him, would be a betrayal to Ry, no matter what Ry had said. She couldn't have feelings for the man. Rosina shook and hugged the pillow tighter. She feared she already had allowed the duke in more than she should have, and the only thing she could do was push aside anything she might feel...forever.

# Chapter 9

Rosina couldn't bear to face James over breakfast after how she reacted to him, so she had Molly request a tray to be brought to her chamber. It was the coward's way out, but she wasn't ready to see him so soon after she had kicked him out of her chamber as he was almost certainly going to express something beyond what their arrangement was supposed to be.

She had cried for a couple hours as the guilt racked her entire body. She could allow herself to admit that she had enjoyed waking up to a man in her bed. No, not just a man, but James. When he called her "Rose" just as Ry used to do, all she could think about was how she had loved Ry with everything she had, and she didn't wish to betray his memory.

And even if she could get past that, her love hadn't been enough to keep him well and with her. She wasn't certain she would survive such a devastating loss again.

Picking at her food, she stared at the plate, feeling more numb than she had in months.

"Are you ready to admit that you have a tendre for the duke?" Molly asked, her tone forceful but caring as she cut into Rosina's thoughts, startling her.

Rosina sighed and her shoulders slumped further. "I believe I shall lie down for a while." She only hoped that Molly would drop the matter as she didn't care at all to speak about it.

Still donning her robe and night rail, she climbed back into her bed and hugged a pillow close to her. The same pillow James had slept on, and the sandalwood scent engulfed her senses, preventing any chance of pushing him from her thoughts.

Ry had said he wanted her to move on and live a full life, but how could she have a full life without him? Was that even possible? Then there was still the very real risk that something could happen to James. Sickness, highwaymen, carriage accidents…any number of things could happen, and her heart wouldn't be able to bear it.

She wasn't certain if she had fallen asleep or not in the time she spent lying in the bed imagining how she would leave the house party and return her life to what it was before she met James. But after some time had passed, she opened her eyes and knew she couldn't lie in bed any longer. There was no way she could hide away in her chamber for the rest of the house party, so she might as well join the others and get the uncomfortable moment with James over with.

Climbing from her bed, she rang for Molly to help her dress. She spotted the dress Molly had left prepared from earlier that morning and removed her robe, dropping it into the nearby chair. After pulling her night rail over her head, she donned a white chemise that was laid by the dress.

Molly came storming into the room without a knock. "You won't believe it, my lady. There has been a fire."

"What? What can you mean?"

"The stables," Molly said, catching her breath. "They went up in flames."

"Was anyone injured?"

Molly moved across the room to where the dress lay waiting. "I'm not certain. I heard a couple of gentlemen ran into the building."

Panic gripped Rosina's heart. "Who?" she demanded. "Which gentlemen?"

"I wasn't told, my lady."

Doing her best to tamp down her fear, she moved quickly to Molly. "Quick. Skip the stays and help me with my dress."

Molly did as she asked and hurried to help button up the dress.

"Just quickly pin my hair up. I must go downstairs and ascertain what has occurred."

Once her hair was pinned in place and she had put on her slippers, she bolted from her room without another word to Molly. She needed to see if James was all right, hoping he hadn't been foolish enough to run into a burning building.

She moved down the grand staircase as quickly as she could. When she reached the foyer, she saw guests congregating in the salon. Glancing from guest to guest, she searched for James. When she didn't see him, her heart raced faster. She searched the corridor and didn't see him there, either.

Moving to the terrace, her breathing was short and quick to match the pace of her heartbeat. At first, she didn't see anyone on the terrace and then a movement in the far corner caught her eye. His back was to her, but she knew it was him. "James." She sighed, briefly closing her eyes in relief.

He spun around to face her. "Rosina." His tone was tinged with trepidation.

"I thought…well, it doesn't matter what I thought," she said. "I am just glad to see you are well."

He eyed her cautiously. "Lord Demming and Lord Knox ran into the stables, but they are both resting in their chambers after all the smoke they inhaled." His expression shifted to one of hope. "I am fine if that is what concerned you."

Rosina released an audible breath and glanced at her feet, shifting herself on them as if she were standing on hot coals. "I'm relieved to hear that."

"Why did you force me out of your chamber?" he asked, almost cutting off her words and taking a few steps closer.

She huffed. "It does not signify."

He took the last few steps towards her and caught her gaze with his intense blue eyes, like that of a stormy sky, that kept her frozen in place. "Everything about you most certainly signifies to me. Tell me, please."

He reached for her hand, and as soon as he clasped it, the ever-present electricity between them shot through her entire body. She pulled it away and glanced around at their surroundings. "We cannot speak here, Your Grace."

James reached for her hand again and clasped tighter that time. He pulled her down the steps of the terrace and through the garden. "Where are we going?"

"You shall see." His tone was one of mirth, which was in stark contrast to his demeanor when they were on the terrace.

Rosina allowed him to lead her beyond the gardens and through a gathering of trees. Once they reached the other side, there was a folly on the other side.

"How did you know this was here?" she asked, being pulled towards the structure.

"I wished to distance myself from the other guests earlier and discovered it."

He pulled her through the opening. The folly was in the shape of a turret that appeared to be a couple of stories high and made of brick. Moss was growing along the outside and there were cutouts for windows that were open to the outside.

"There," he continued. "We are quite alone. So now you shall tell me what upset you this morning."

She wrapped her arms around herself. "I woke up to find a man in my bed. I was alarmed."

"I think there is more to it than that. You told me not to call you 'Rose', and then you became upset."

Rosina drew a deep breath and turned away from him. She glanced at the tall ceiling of the folly and then took a few more steadying breaths. Shifting her gaze down to the floor, she responded, "Ry called me Rose."

"Rosina," he started, his tone pained as he turned her to face him again. "I didn't know. I'm so sorry."

"I know you didn't. I just felt…" her voice trailed off.

He cupped her cheek with his hand. "What did you feel?"

"Ry was the only man I had ever shared a bed with in that way."

"I'm sorry," he said quickly. "I shouldn't have done so."

She shook her head. "You don't understand. I enjoyed it."

He contemplated her. "And that makes you feel guilty." He didn't pose it as a question, nor did he appear to be irritated by the revelation.

"I don't know what I feel, James."

He wrapped his arms around her and pulled her against him, almost causing her to go weak in the knees from his embrace.

"But you feel something?" The tone in the way he asked was almost pleading.

James lowered his lips towards hers and stopped just before they would touch, waiting for her to give some kind of response. She gave a few small nods, and he pressed his lips to hers. Deepening the kiss, he swept his tongue into her mouth and massaged hers with such intensity that she became dependent on his hold on her to remain standing.

"I want you, James," she whispered, breaking their kiss.

He released a low growl and picked her up so that she wrapped her legs around his waist, then took her lips again. Walking towards the nearest wall, he pressed her back to it to help anchor her against him. The cool brick beneath the fabric of her dress warred with the heat of his hard body against her front.

Working his hand beneath her skirts, he brushed his fingers across her slit, causing her to release a series of moans.

James slipped two fingers inside of her cunt. "I am pleased you are so wet, as I can hardly wait."

She watched as he removed his fingers and began working the buttons of his falls to free himself. As soon as his cock jutted between them, he lifted her over himself and then lowered her to take all of him.

"You feel so bloody perfect," he whispered against her ear before licking and sucking along the sensitive part of her neck.

Rosina rocked against him as much as she could with the wall supporting her back, and he groaned. He thrust into her, gripping her hips to hold her in place against the wall. Tightening her legs around his waist as he bucked harder, his breathing ragged from the exertion.

She removed one hand that had been around his neck and slipped it between them to massage her pearl while he took her.

"Yes," he ground out. "Touch yourself. Lift your skirts higher so I can watch."

Releasing his neck, she did as he said and bunched her skirts with her other hand so we could see her hand at work.

He slowed his thrusts and kept his gaze trained on her hand, releasing a series of low growls and moans as she panted from bringing herself closer and closer to a sweet release.

Steadily increasing his speed, he thrust harder into her. He entered her so deep with his entire length, and she became more undone each time he did so. When her orgasm hit, it consumed her entire body. She rocked and cried out his name with abandon since no one would hear them.

James pulled her off him, set her to stand before him, then took himself in hand to stroke his shaft, closing his eyes. She dropped to her knees on the stone floor and sucked the head of his cock into her mouth.

"Fuck," he whispered, clasping her head in his hands and pushing himself deeper into her mouth.

Rosina cupped his ballocks with her hand and massaged them while she sucked hard down the base of his length.

He growled and pulled back, then thrust again. She didn't relent on how she sucked him, and he thrust one more time before he spent his warm seed on her tongue.

As soon as she had swallowed what he gave her, he reached for her and pulled her to stand before him, then placed a few tender kisses at the corner of her lips.

"Rosina," he whispered, resting his forehead against hers while they both caught their breaths. "What is happening between us?"

"I don't know." That much was true.

"What do you want it all to mean?"

"I truly don't know, James." Another truth. "Can we just enjoy each other for now?" She trembled, still uncertain she could allow herself to accept her feelings. When she had said she wanted him, she didn't just mean physically, but admitting that to him would only start them on a path she wasn't certain she wished to be on.

He pulled back and gave her a soft smile. "Of course," he replied, then shifted his expression to a smirk. "Minx."

# Chapter 10

James had lost his heart to the beautiful Lady Preston, and he wasn't certain she would ever let her walls down enough to allow a future for them. He was the fool who allowed himself to feel more for her. The arrangement was only supposed to be about pleasure, but somehow he had fallen in love with her along the way.

She wasn't just beautiful, though she was most definitely that, but she was also confident and fierce. Everything he could want for his duchess and the woman who would be at his side for the rest of his life. When had he started thinking about forevers and happily-ever-afters?

After their time in the folly, he visited her chamber that evening and she ensured they were far too preoccupied to do much talking. Although he longed to know what she might feel for him.

He shook off his thoughts and continued reading one of the recent newspapers. After breakfast that morning, Rosina took off with her friend, Lady Lily, and James decided it might be best to give the lady a bit of space. Perhaps he didn't truly know his own mind. He was only three-and-twenty, too young by the standards of most to consider marrying so soon. Besides, he had his brothers to consider. They needed him.

Continuing to read the paper, he did his best to push thoughts of Rosina out of his mind. He read about the latest news for another quarter hour until he became restless and decided he could no longer sit in the high-backed chair in the Ockhams' drawing room.

Coming to a stand, he placed the paper on the table and then stretched his shoulders. Before he could stop himself, he wondered where Rosina was and fought to think of an excuse for why he needed to remain by her side, even though he knew he shouldn't. He was nothing more than a besotted fool. That dratted Demming had been right.

"Your Grace," the Ockhams' butler, Baxter, said, effectively pulling him from his thoughts. "There is a matter that requires your attention."

James eyed the man curiously, uncertain of what he might be needed for. "What matter?"

"If you will come with me, your grace," Baxter said, motioning for him to follow.

James did as the man asked and followed him down the corridor and to the foyer.

"Brother!" a familiar voice called, and before he knew it, he had two sets of small arms wrapped around him.

"What in the devil are you two doing here?" He practically shouted his question. "How did you get here?"

"Please don't be mad, Brother," Walter said, pleading with him. "William's bad dreams returned and he was frightened. He needed to see you."

James' expression softened, but before he could speak, Baxter stepped in. "I shall alert her ladyship to the arrival of our guests and see that a room can be made up for them. At least for tonight."

"I would appreciate that," James said, nodding his appreciation to the man. "Please give my apologies to her ladyship for the inconvenience." He made a mental note as Baxter took off that he would also need to express his gratitude to his hosts once he determined what his brothers were about.

Looking down at his brothers, who still had him in a tight embrace, he wriggled out of their grasp. "Come with me. We shall discuss the matter in my chamber."

He led the boys up the staircase, then to the right to the wing where his chamber had been assigned. Opening the door, he ushered them inside the room and then closed it behind them. They each rushed over to the settee and plopped onto it beside each other, looking up at him expectantly.

James dropped himself into the chair across from them. "Now tell me about this bad dream of yours, William."

"It was awful, James. I dreamt you were attacked on the way to this house party like Mama and Papa." He sniffled as he spoke. "And then I dreamt the same thing again. I was worried something had happened to you."

His heart broke that his brother had been racked with fear, but leaving school wasn't acceptable.

"You should have spoken with your teachers, and they would have contacted me. You know I would have come straight away. Boys, you can't leave on your own with no one aware of where you are. All manner of bad things could have happened to you both. You understand that, don't you?"

Walter and William each gave him somber nods. "We're sorry, James," Walter said.

"I don't want you to do something like this again, ever," James said, sounding more like a parent than a brother, so he softened his expression slightly. "I shall write to your school so they know where you are, and then we will make plans to return you there."

"James, please," William started. "Can't we just stay with you? You can hire us tutors like we did before. We don't need to go to school."

He could see how William trembled, and he rushed over to his brothers and knelt before them. "Do you both feel that way?"

William nodded, but Walter hesitated a bit before also giving him a nod. Each of their faces was in a pout that reminded him of when he had to tell them about their parents. He knew they needed to be at school and knew the three of them couldn't spend every day together for the rest of their lives, but he couldn't bear to cause them any more pain.

"Very well," he said, questioning if he was making the right decision. "You may return home with me." If only their parents were still alive, and none of them would be in such a position. The boys would be away happily at school, making friends and having the time of their lives.

"Thank you! Thank you!" each of the boys exclaimed, throwing their arms around his neck. He hugged them back.

"I need you both to be on your best behavior until I confirm when we shall depart," James said, eyeing each of them.

"We will, Brother, we promise," William said.

He hugged them again, but suddenly, an image of Rosina flashed into his mind. There would be nothing more between them once he left. She already barely let him in, and once he departed, she would harden her heart towards him completely. It was a very real possibility he wouldn't even see her again. His heart fractured in his chest, and he released a sad sigh.

"What is wrong, Brother?" Walter said, eyeing him curiously.

"It's nothing." He lied to his brothers. Because it was everything.

Thankfully, Lord and Lady Ockham were understanding about the situation with his brothers. He sent the necessary correspondence to the school so they wouldn't worry about where the boys went. He spent the afternoon with them, listening to their stories about their studies and some of the friends they had made.

It sounded to James like they had enjoyed school until William had suffered from the nightmares. If that hadn't occurred, he had a feeling the boys would still be happily away at school. It also explained why James hadn't received a letter from them yet, as they had been busy with their new friends. He questioned his decision to allow them to remain at home instead of going to school, but he could think on that later once they all had more time to discuss the matter.

They didn't encounter Rosina when he took the boys on a stroll through the gardens to show them the estate. He showed them where the fire had occurred at the stables and used the opportunity to remind them of how destructive fires could be. And why it was so important to be mindful of any kind of flame.

For dinner that evening, he had requested trays for them all to be brought to the chamber where the boys were staying. It was only a couple of doors down from him, which made things convenient to keep an eye on them.

After they finished their meal and the trays had been taken away, he settled the boys into their beds. He figured they would most likely depart the following day to not be a burden on their hosts. A country house party wasn't exactly the place for a pair of boys their age.

Once he bid them good night, he returned to his own chamber. The house was quiet, but given the time, he was certain there were still guests lingering about. Then there would be the guests who would swap their chambers for the evening. The way he had done with Rosina.

He wanted to go to her that evening. More than anything. By then she had to have heard about his brothers' arrival, as such a thing would be known quickly amongst the entire party. And if they hadn't spread the news, his disappearance from the party would cause talk on its own.

James paced his room. He needed to speak with her before he left, but what would we say? Could he tell her he loved her but he had to go? Could he beg her to love him, too, and consider a life with him? He was almost certain she would decline that offer before he could even finish the words, and then where would that leave him?

There were the boys to consider as well. If William was having nightmares, adjusting to the notion of James marrying and adding someone else to their family was a risk. If the boys would even accept her at all. But could he live the rest of his life without her? Or without at least trying to win her?

The sound of his chamber door clicking closed reached his ears and his chin jerked in that direction. Expecting to see one of the boys, he was surprised to see Rosina leaning against the closed door.

"How did you know this was my chamber?" He mentally chastised himself for asking such a pointless question. Who really cared how she came across the information?

"I asked."

"Why did you come?" He didn't bother hiding the hope in his tone, and that was a far more important question.

She took a few steps closer to where he sat in the chair before the fireplace. "I heard about your brothers, and I wanted to see if you were all right."

He flashed her a playful grin. "So you were thinking about me?"

James was almost certain she had rolled her eyes at him. "I suppose," she said.

"I believe I shall depart with the boys tomorrow," he blurted, hoping her reaction might be one of sadness or longing.

"I see."

No such luck.

"I'm not ready to depart from you," he said, deciding to bare just a bit of his heart to her.

She moved another few steps closer, and he could see her better with the light from the fire dancing across her features. The sadness was there, and it caused his heart to catch in his throat.

"Me neither, Duke."

He leapt from his chair and captured her in his arms, holding her close to him. "Come with me," he pleaded.

She pulled back, and she eyed him as if he belonged in Bedlam. "Are you mad? I can't just come with you."

"Why not?" He leaned forward and placed a tender kiss on her lips before trailing kisses along her jaw. "Marry me, Rosina," he whispered against her ear. "As much as I promised I wouldn't, and then tried not to. I love you."

"James," she whispered, nuzzling her cheek against his. "I can't."

His heart shattered into little pieces, and his entire body recoiled from her rejection. James released her. "Why?"

"I…I just…James…"

He watched her stammer with her words and awaited what blow she might deliver. Did she truly not care for him at all?

William's voice cut through Rosina's broken words. "Brother?"

# Chapter 11

Rosina was unsure how to tell James that she was almost certain she loved him, too, but that she couldn't bear the thought of admitting it and then living a life in fear that she would lose him. She believed suffering from that pain would be far worse than the pain of walking away from him.

Before she could answer him, a young boy appeared in the room, followed by another, who looked almost identical to the first.

"What are you boys doing up?" James asked.

The boys stepped further into the room and closed the door behind them. "We couldn't sleep."

Once she got a better look at them, she saw how both boys also looked very similar to James. It would be undeniable to anyone that the trio were brothers.

"Come here, boys," James said, waving them over. He placed an arm around each of their shoulders. "Boys, I'd like you to meet Lady Preston." He shifted his attention to Rosina, and an amused expression played on his lips. "These scamps are my brothers, William and Walter."

They each gave her a quick bow.

"I'm pleased to meet the both of you," she replied. "You must have had quite the journey to seek out your brother."

"Are you married, Lady Preston?" Walter asked. "It's not proper for you to be in our brother's chamber when you are married."

She wouldn't point out that it wasn't proper for her to be in their brother's chamber at all. Rosina drew a deep breath. "I was married before. But he died three years ago."

Walter frowned. "I'm sorry, my lady. You must be very sad and miss him. We still miss our mama and papa very much."

"I'm also very sorry about your mother and father. It's a fortunate thing that you have your brother." She already adored the earnest, charming boys. She could see so much of James in them and the influence he had in ensuring they were loved and cared for.

"We are returning home together tomorrow," William said. "James said we can live with him and not return to school."

She eyed them curiously. "Why wouldn't you wish to return to school? Did something happen?"

"We would rather be with James," Walter said, answering for his brother.

Rosina wasn't certain that was the right choice for the boys, nor if James would wish to have her opinion on the matter. "Did you not enjoy school?"

"Oh, we did, very much," Walter said. "We made so many friends, and our teachers have said we are excelling in all our studies. The food there isn't as good as Cook's, but it's still quite good. We still get to ride when we want and play various sports with the other boys."

They seemed to enjoy school, so their desire to leave made little sense to her. She caught James' gaze, and he only wore a frown.

"Then why ever would you wish to return home?" Rosina asked. "It sounds as if you are doing quite well, indeed."

William opened his mouth to speak but hesitated. Rosina moved to the settee and encouraged the boys to come and sit with her. She had always enjoyed children and had longed to have her own. It surprised her when the boys followed her so quickly, each taking a seat on either side of her.

James took a seat in the chair across from them, appearing just as surprised as she was based on how wide his eyes were, watching the scene unfold.

They sat in silence for a few moments before William finally spoke. "I'm afraid something will happen to James if we aren't here."

"Because of what happened to your parents?" she asked softly.

He nodded and gave a small sniffle.

She shifted her attention to Walter. "And are you also afraid?"

Walter contemplated her question. "A little bit. Not as much as William is, but I don't want anything to happen to James. He's all we have left."

Rosina glanced at James and saw that his eyes had become watery, and he gripped the armrests of the chair to fight his emotion. She was almost certain she was overstepping her place, but it was clear that the trio needed a bit of help to move past the matter and help the boys see they needed to be in school.

"I can tell you adore your brother dearly, as I am sure he does you. But you can't live your life in fear of the things you can't control. That wouldn't be a life worth living." She contemplated her own words, and her heart swelled. "Your parents would want you to live a full life, and that includes going to school and making friends. And one day you'll take wives, and you'll settle into your own homes." For the first time, she almost understood why Ry had told her what he did, pleaded with her even, and why he wished for her to find happiness again.

The boys appeared to truly ponder what she said as their brows furrowed and unfurrowed.

She continued, "You will still see your brother for holidays and summers, and if you need him to visit you, I am sure he will do so. Perhaps you might even write him a letter now and then." She hunched down and pretended that she was whispering, even though she intended for James to hear her. "He was quite a mess waiting for a letter to arrive from you two."

William jerked his head towards James. "Is that true, Brother?"

James just nodded, still fighting to keep himself together in front of them all. "Mm–hm."

Walter leaned forward to get William's attention. "I think we should go back to school."

"I do, too," William replied, then looked at James again. "Is that all right, Brother? Can we still go back to school after all, if we promise we will write to you each week?"

James grinned, and it warmed Rosina's full heart. "Of course. I'll expect those letters, though."

Unexpectedly, the boys each wrapped their arms around her. She patted them as best as she could with her arms pinned.

"Are you going to marry James?" William asked. "We heard him ask you."

"I…uh…I'm uncertain." She also wasn't certain what to say or how she felt about the matter. The advice she had given to the boys could directly apply to herself, but could she throw caution to the wind and give her heart to James?

"Don't you love him?" Walter asked.

"Boys," James called out in warning.

Walter ignored his brother's warning. "If you married James, you wouldn't have to be sad about your first husband any longer." If only it were that simple.

"And James wouldn't be so lonely waiting for our letters," William added. "And you could keep an eye on him and make sure he's safe."

She put her arms around each of them, finding that the two boys were quite easy to become attached to. "Are you trying to say that you wish for me to marry your brother?"

"Yes!" the boys said in unison.

"Boys," James said, rising from his seat. "I won't have you pressuring the lady to marry me. If she does so, it will be because of her own choice. Now let's get you two back to bed so I might discuss the matter with her privately."

He waved them to him. They each gave Rosina a quick hug before they followed their brother to the door. James glanced back over his shoulder at her. "Wait here. Please."

It was her chance. She could escape to her chamber and lock her door and never have to face him again if she wished. But she didn't want to. And that revelation was enough to aid in her choice to stay. To see if she might overcome her own fear.

James returned a few moments later and locked the door behind him after he entered.

"I'm really sorry about that," he said, crossing the room to take a seat beside her on the settee.

"Don't be. They are wonderful boys."

He took her hand in his. "They adore you. I can't say I blame them."

The silence hung between them for a few moments until he finally spoke again. "Why did you say no to my offer?"

"I'm afraid." It was the simplest, truest answer.

He pulled her closer and moved his arm around her. She noted how she wasn't even tempted to move away and instead sank into him, absorbing all the love that radiated from his touch.

"What are you afraid of, sweetheart?"

"Everything," she whispered. "I'm afraid that the more of my heart I give to you that it will completely erase the memory of Ry. And I'm afraid that you will be upset that I could love you and still have days where I miss him. He wasn't just my husband, James, he was my best friend. As much as I know I can't control such things, I'm also afraid I will allow myself to love you completely and then you will be taken away from me, too."

James cupped both of her cheeks with his hands. Tears streamed down them and were caught by his thumbs. "I would never ask you to forget about him or the part of your life that you shared. I'm not so insecure in my affection for you that I don't understand the complexity of the matter. Loving him made you the woman that I love. I just hope you will allow us a chance at happiness, and perhaps make some room in your heart to love me, too."

She began to cry, and he pulled her against him, holding her so lovingly that it only made her weep harder. "I do love you, James," she sobbed into his coat.

He rubbed her back and let her cry. "I'm sorry I broke our rules, but I'm not sorry that I fell in love with you," he said softly. When she sat up to look at him through her lashes, he wiped her eyes for her. "Does that mean you will marry me?"

She drew a deep breath and told herself to be the bold woman she had always been and go after what she wanted. And what she wanted was to be married to the man before her. To bear his children and to care for his sweet little brothers who needed their love and guidance.

"Yes."

He picked her up and set her in his lap before kissing her with such intensity she believed he feared he might never have the chance to do so again. She returned his kiss with the same need, hoping to convey everything she felt for him at that moment.

When he broke the kiss, he held her tight and pressed his forehead to hers. "Will you depart with me tomorrow?"

"Tongues will wag if I do so."

"Let them say a word about it. They will live to regret it when I cut each and every one of them and have everyone we know do the same."

She laughed. "Glad to know you haven't gone completely soft from love, Duke. There are times when I certainly prefer you to be the commanding duke, Your Grace."

Dark desire flashed across his handsome visage, and she knew he understood her meaning. He quickly unbuttoned his falls to release himself and then shifted her so that she straddled him, his cock protruding proudly between them. Raising her skirts, he began working his hands between her thighs.

"Take all of my cock, my future duchess."

If his fingers hadn't already made her more than ready for him, his words certainly would have. He lifted her and helped her slide down on top of him. He released a low groan when she was fully seated, and she reveled in the effect she had on him.

She rocked her hips hard against him. Placing her hands behind her on his knees, she leaned back so she pleasured them both from a different angle. It was met with approval from the way he bucked and growled beneath her, gripping her hips to aid in moving her faster.

He shifted one of his hands to her breasts, lowering the neckline of her dress so they each hung out of the front, bobbing with each of her movements to ride his shaft. He massaged her right breast and gave her nipple a gentle squeeze.

She was so close to her release, each time she seated herself on him, she brought herself closer to the brink of ecstasy.

"Love, I am so close…" he ground out, his words low and gravelly.

"Do you wish for me to stop?" she asked, slowing her movements.

"Not anymore," he replied quickly.

She leaned forward and kissed him, sweeping her tongue into his mouth. Then she pulled back so they were nose to nose. "I don't either."

"If I release inside of you, there is no backing out. You are marrying me," he said, gripping her hips again. She loved how her skin heated everywhere he touched her.

"Nothing could stop me," she said, increasing the speed of her hips.

"I love you so much," he said between breaths.

She rocked against him in a steady rhythm. "I love you, too, James."

He groaned, his breathing ragged, and he thrust upwards into her.

The first wave of her orgasm hit her, and she clenched and slowed to drag out every second as it expanded to send pulses through her entire body. James gripped her hips and held her down against him as he pumped into her, moaning her name as he filled her with his seed.

She slumped against him, tired and sated from the exertion, placing soft kisses on his jaw before burying her face in his neck.

James lovingly wrapped his arms around her. "Is there anything you wish to command me to do, my future wife?"

She thought for a moment and then nuzzled her nose against his chin. "You will allow me to sleep in your bed tonight and to depart with you tomorrow."

Pulling herself up so she could face him, she found that he was smirking at her.

"That's my good little minx."

# Epilogue

## 3 MONTHS LATER

Rosina moved about the house, directing everyone on where to place the greenery they had all gone out to collect. They used the greenery to make wreaths, garlands, and kissing balls, complete with mistletoe.

Lily and her husband, Alex, Viscount Callan, came to stay with them for the holidays, so the house was full of love and laughter, especially with the boys home from school.

William and Walter couldn't contain their excitement when they found out she had agreed to marry their brother, and she believed it might make them reconsider their decision to return to school. They had agreed to keep the boys with them long enough to procure a special license and marry right away, with the boys in attendance.

Once they dropped the boys off at school, they consummated their marriage in the carriage, which still made her skin heat and dampness pool between her thighs when she thought about that particular encounter, their first as husband and wife.

"Sweetheart, you should be taking it easy," James said, taking a few kissing balls from her hand as she was attempting to hang them.

"Duke, we have at least seven months to go, and one can hardly tell I am increasing. You will have plenty of time to encourage me to rest."

He hung one of the kissing balls where she had been working. "Well, you have only just started keeping your breakfast down again. Besides, it's my job to keep you both safe."

"I tell Lily the same thing," Alex cut in, coming back for more decorations to hang.

"And I allow you to carry me about, no matter how ridiculous it is," Lily responded.

It was a relief that Alex and James had become fast friends since it enabled Lily and Rosina to see each other as often as they could, and they would have their babes around the same time.

"Sister," William called to Rosina, "can we have some of the gingerbread? Everything is hung up like you asked."

She grinned at them both. "Certainly. Thank you for your help."

James and she had agreed that they would give the boys a grand Christmas since next year they would have a new babe join the family. They wanted this one to be special for the boys and focus on giving them all the love and attention they could handle, especially while they still wanted it. They were becoming more independent by the day, and it was only a matter of time before they'd beg to go to their friends' homes for holidays and breaks.

Later that evening, they enjoyed a Christmas Eve feast fit for the king himself, then gathered in the drawing room together to sing carols. The fire roared in the fireplace, and on the mantle were three candles that the boys lit. One for their mother, one for their father, and one for Ryan. She had cried and clutched the boys to her when they told her what they wished to do. It was something they had done to remember their parents each year since their passing, and it touched her heart that they thought to do the same for Ry. It could have been at James' suggestion, but she would never ask.

She pressed the keys of the pianoforte as everyone sang along, the candles on the mantle catching her eye. Almost immediately, she glanced over at her husband and found him staring back at her. All the love in the world shone in his expression.

There wasn't a day since they married that she regretted allowing herself to love him. It wasn't the same as what she felt for Ry, nor was it better or worse, or stronger or lesser. It just was. She loved James with her entire heart and everything she had, and she was also thankful for the time she had to love Ry. She realized that both loves could be true.

Her family had been ecstatic and astonished to find out that she had wed the Duke of St. Albans. They weren't certain about referring to him as "James" the first time they met him, but he'd used his haughty duke tone with them, and that was that.

They would all arrive in a few days to spend some time together as one big family. Her mother wrote that she was bringing a few gifts for the boys, as they had been welcomed into the family as if Rosina had birthed them herself. James and his brothers deserved to have a bit of family who adored them to make up for what they had so tragically lost. She supposed she did, too.

Her heart overflowing with happiness, she mouthed, "I love you," to her husband, whose gaze was fixed on her.

Once the evening had ended, everyone went upstairs to bed. The boys were excited about Christmas morning and what surprises might wait for them.

Rosina blew out the candles on the mantle, knowing the boys would relight them tomorrow, and turned to find her husband standing in front of the closed door.

"You have that look in your eye, Duke."

"Whatever do you mean?" he asked, giving her a coy expression. Then he slinked over to her like a lion stalking his prey.

She laughed and folded her arms across her body. "You know exactly what I mean."

He grabbed her and pulled her tight against him, walking her backwards towards the fire. He pulled one of the kissing balls from behind him and held it over her head.

Grinning at him, she clutched the lapels of his coat and pulled him to her, then took his lips in a searing kiss. She would never tire of kissing her perfect husband. Even if it was scandalous to do so in their drawing room when they had guests in their home.

He scooped her up and crouched to the floor with her, laying her before the fire. Raising her skirts to bunch at her waist, he moved his fingers against her slit, knowing he was driving her to distraction.

"I wish to kiss you here." He lazily circled her nub with his fingers.

"You don't need a kissing ball to do so."

He said nothing further and shifted so his head was between her legs, licking and sucking at her pearl, while he sheathed two fingers inside of her cunt. It didn't take long before she was bucking and moaning, pushing herself against his face to ride the last wave of pleasure.

While she lay basking before the fire from the bliss his wicked mouth delivered, he had undone his falls and settled between her legs. He brought the fingers that had been inside of her to his lips and sucked them into his mouth. "So sweet. Far better than any gingerbread."

She moaned and rubbed herself against him, urging him to enter her.

"I believe my wife needs a taste." He again pushed his fingers inside of her and then withdrew them, bringing them to her lips. She sucked them into her mouth at the same time he thrust his cock all the way inside of her to the hilt. Rosina responded by wrapping her legs around him to hold him in place against her.

James mimicked the speed of his movements with the way she moved to suck his fingers, groaning each time she took them deep into her mouth, allowing them to brush the back of her throat.

He removed his fingers from her mouth and ran his hand along her body until he reached her hip. Lifting her hip slightly so he could enter her deeper with each thrust.

For a man who was a virgin only three months prior, he had quickly become an expert in how to bring her the most intense pleasure.

His thrusts were slow and deep, taking his time to bring them both to the pinnacle of their desire. They were both panting and moaning, clinging to each other in their rapture while the light from the fire kissed their skin.

She slowly fell over the exquisite edge of her climax, digging her fingers into his coat, moaning through the orgasm that seemed to last for minutes. It appeared to be the same for him as he whispered her name and fought for his breath as he rocked into her, filling her.

James went limp and lay beside her, pulling her with him. "I love you, Duchess."

Still trying to catch her breath, she kissed the tip of his nose. "I love you, Duke."

Placing his hand on her stomach, he rubbed over the fabric of her dress. "I don't think life could get any better than this. You, our babe, the boys, our family and friends. We are quite lucky, indeed."

"Well," she said in a teasing tone. "Perhaps we shall have twins."

## Want more of James and Rosina?

They have appearances in the other books in the Unlikely Betrothal series! If you haven't met Nick and Eliza from *The Earl and the Vixen,* get your copy today!

Here is a look at the full series, and keep reading for a sneak peek at *The Earl and the Vixen*!

## The Unlikely Betrothal Series

A different couple at the same house party finds their match! Who will be next? Each of these books are stand-alone stories complete with a HEA and lots of spice, but recommended reading order is below:

The Earl and the Vixen

The Rake and the Muse

The Marquess and the Earl

The Viscount and the Wallflower

The Duke and the Widow

# Dearest Reader

Thank you for taking the time to read *The Duke and the Widow*! I hope you enjoyed this spicy read from my Unlikely Betrothal series. I enjoyed bringing James and Rosina's story to life on the page and can't wait to introduce you to the other couples at the Ockhams' house party!

I am so thankful for all my readers and would appreciate it if you would leave an honest review on sites like Amazon, Goodreads, BookBub, etc.! Also, I'd love to stay in touch, so please visit christinadianebooks.com to join my mailing list and receive a free copy of Only A Rake Will Do (the Ockhams are in that one, too!), and stay informed on upcoming releases, promotions, and current projects.

If you are interested in being on my permanent ARC team and/or Street Team, send me a message on one of my socials! I'd love to chat!

I hope all of you will follow me and get the latest happenings and info on releases from my historical romance friends on any of my socials:

- Website: christinadianebooks.com

- Substack: @christinadianeauthor

- The Desire Den Discord

- Instagram: @christinadianeauthor

- Facebook: christinadiane

- TikTok: @christinadianeauthor

- YouTube: @ChristinaDianeAuthor

- BlueSky: @christinadiane.bsky.social

- Twitter: @CDianeAuthor

- GoodReads: ChristinaDiane

- Follow Me on Amazon: Christina Diane

- Follow Me onBookBub: <u>Christina Diane</u>

- Join my Reader Group: <u>The Swoonworthy Scoundrels Society</u>

- Join my other Author Group: <u>Society of Smut & Scandal</u>

Hopefully I left you wanting more, so keep reading for a sneak peek *The Earl and the Vixen* from the Unlikely Betrothal series! You can also go ahead and get a full copy of *The Earl and the Vixen* in paperback, ebook, and audio!

# The Earl and the Vixen

## SURREY, ENGLAND - SPRING 1810

"I love you, Eliza, and I intend to marry you. To hell with our fathers. Please tell me you want to be with me as much as I wish to be with you. In every way."

Elizabeth Nelson, the eldest daughter of the Earl of Nelson, melted into the arms of her sweetheart, Nicholas, who would one day become the Earl of Craven. She had loved him from the first time she'd come across him swimming in the stream that ran between their fathers' estates, almost five years ago.

Although the ownership of that very stream had been a long-disputed issue between their fathers. They each believed that the stream belonged to them and made trouble for each other when either household made use of it for livestock or to provide irrigation to crops. Ultimately, they both ended up using it for their estates anyway, and one would think they could be content with that. But a silly stream had been enough to cause such a rift that the men had sworn to hate each other. The bad blood only became worse between the pair over the years.

When she first saw Nick all those years ago, he hadn't given one whit about her back then. She had been far too young, and he had only been home for the summer from Eton, and by the time fall came again, he was gone. When he returned years later, he came across her reading a novel by the very same stream and finally noticed her, a woman and no longer an annoying young chit. They spent the next few months falling more in love each day and taking a few scandalous swims together at night in the stream in a rebellious slight against their fathers.

There wasn't a doubt in her mind that she wished to marry him, and she wanted nothing more than to give him every part of herself. To truly become his and make him hers. As a young woman of eight-and-ten whom no one spoke of such things to, she knew very little of what that would mean, but she knew she only wished to experience such things with Nick.

He would have offered to marry her already, and they would already be betrothed if they knew for certain how their fathers would react. Given the hatred the men harbored for each other, they feared that Eliza's father wouldn't agree to the union. With her age, they needed his approval to do so properly, or they would have to do something scandalous like elope to Gretna Green.

"I love you, too," she said, burying her face in his neck. "I want very much to be with you, Nick."

He took her mouth with his, kissing her with fervent intensity. When he broke the kiss, he brought her hands to his swollen lips. "Meet me at the hunting cabin tonight, after it is dark. We can be alone there, just the two of us with no one to disturb us."

She looked at their hands, attempting to mask her frown.

"What is it, Eliza? If you have doubts, we can wait," Nick said. He lifted her chin to meet his mesmerizing green eyes. His chestnut hair was just a bit longer than was fashionable, and it made him all the more roguish and handsome. "Look at me. I mean it, if this isn't something you wish to do—"

"It's not that," she said, cutting him off.

"Then is it something I have done? Did you not enjoy when I touched you…" his voice trailed off as he gestured towards her skirts.

"It is most certainly not that either," she said before swallowing hard. She had quite enjoyed it when he introduced her to the most exquisite pleasure she had ever experienced. "It's just that I know you have experienced these things before, and I haven't a clue what to expect or what to do."

Nick had always been honest with her, and he told her of his time at Cambridge and that there had been women who warmed his bed. He spared her the details, which she appreciated, but she wasn't so secure in herself that it didn't spark a flicker of jealousy, especially when she was about to lay herself bare before him.

She knew that the rules of society were different for men than women, especially since Nick was two-and-twenty and exposed to the things men do while at university, but it didn't mean she had to like it.

He cupped her cheek with his hand. "My love, you will be perfect. All I need is you. The rest we can explore together."

"But you—"

"Nothing that happened before you matters," he said, cutting her off, "and I know it isn't fair for me to say so, but I would be driven mad if I had to imagine even the mere notion of another man touching you. If I could change the past, I promise you, I would. Just know that it is of little import to me. You are my future. My every-thing."

She pressed onto her toes and kissed him again. "I will meet you tonight. I shall have to wait until after Papa goes to bed if I hope to leave." Her papa would not approve of her sneaking out to meet any man, let alone the son of the Earl of Craven. He might have apoplexy if he knew she intended to give Nick her virtue. Papa tolerated Nick's presence when he came to call only because of the polite-ness society expected. She was certain Papa would refuse him if it wouldn't upset Eliza. Perhaps when she and Nick married, their fathers might resolve things between them. One could only hope.

He brought her hand to his lips again and kissed her knuckles. "You had better return home before someone comes looking for us," he said. "I will see you tonight, my love."

She took his lips again for a few quick pecks and peeked around the corner from the back of her family's stables, ensuring no one could see her as she hurried back towards the house. Her father might tolerate Nick visiting for tea, but if he caught her with him unchaperoned, she wasn't certain she'd see the light of day again. They had to get creative to find ways to sneak off without her maid in tow.

Eliza made it back to the terrace of her grand country home without anyone taking notice. As soon as she entered, she almost walked straight into her father.

"Where have you been, daughter?" he asked.

"I was just taking in the air in the garden, Papa," she lied. She didn't enjoy lying to her father, but she couldn't have him locking her away in her room. Surely love was a reason to justify the minor sin.

His brow furrowed, assessing her. "Where is your maid? You shouldn't be roaming the grounds alone."

"You are quite right, Papa. I just stepped out for a few moments after I was tired of reading. I will make sure Dot goes with me next time," she said, hoping her father wouldn't press her any further.

"Very well. See that you do. Did that boy call here today?"

"Nick?" she asked.

Her father nodded. "And shouldn't you refer to him as Lord Craven?" Hate spewed when her father spoke the title. "You aren't on familiar terms."

Eliza opted not to point out that her father should also refer to Nick by his title and not "that boy," but she opted to leave that unsaid. "Papa, he isn't his father and has done nothing to you. And no, he didn't," she replied. It wasn't exactly a lie since he didn't come calling to their door. "Perhaps he will come for tea tomorrow."

"You are to depart for town with your mama in a few weeks for the season. You are certain to marry before the season ends, so there isn't much point in the boy calling here, I should think," he said, his lips curled into a smirk.

"Perhaps he will offer for me and save you the expense of a season, Papa," she said, testing the waters for her father's reaction.

If she hoped to find a hint of his thoughts on her statement, she would be disappointed. His expression remained unchanged, other than a slight squint of his eyes.

"Perhaps," he said, "but you would have many acceptable options if you had a season."

She patted her father's arm. "The most important thing is that I marry someone who loves me, right, Papa?"

"And someone who is respectable and comes from an excellent family. Someone who would ensure you are provided for," her father said, his cool expression still unchanged.

"Of course, Papa," she replied. "I should like to return to the new book I just purchased with my pin money. May I be excused?" She wasn't ready to tell her father she had already made her choice and would marry Nick. Even if she had to run away with him to Gretna, he was the man she would marry, and there wasn't a thing her father could do about it.

"See you at dinner," her father said before departing towards his study.

Eliza continued to her room, unable to concentrate on reading as her heart wouldn't stop racing. She couldn't wait for her rendezvous with Nick later that evening, where she would learn what it meant to couple with the man she loved.

Around eleven o'clock, Eliza poked her head out of her room to see if anyone was lurking in the hallway. Dot had dressed her for bed a couple hours ago and set her hair into a long plait held in place with a ribbon before she sent the maid away for the evening. Eliza slipped on a serviceable day dress over her night rail and then covered herself with a pelisse to help keep from catching a chill in the cool night air.

Once she was certain there was no one moving about the house, she slipped out of her room and closed the door behind her. She made her way downstairs and snuck out via the door the servants used to access the kitchen garden.

The hunting cabin was only a ten-minute swift ride away, and she knew the route well. With a confident smile, she set off on the journey, assured of her safety under the luminous full moon. She crept to the mews, and a groom greeted her.

"Please saddle up my horse and tell no one that you saw me," she said, handing him a couple of coins.

He pocketed the coins and set off to do as she asked. Jimmy had done so for her a few times before, when she would sneak out to see Nick. The last time they snuck to the hunting cabin, she learnt what an orgasm was. Who knew that a man's hands could give such pleasure? She clenched her thighs together, already thinking about what delights he would introduce her to that evening.

A few moments later, Jimmy handed her the reins, positioning the horse by the mounting block. She thanked him and climbed into the saddle before flicking the reins and racing off into the night.

When she reached the cabin, Nick's horse was already tied up outside. He waited on the porch for her and came right beside her horse and lifted her down. "I'm so very glad you made it, my love. I would have preferred to escort you," Nick said, pulling her into an embrace for a quick kiss. "Let's get you inside. I already started a fire for us."

She grabbed his hand, and he led her inside. The warmth from the fire kissed her skin right away. She removed her pelisse and laid it across the back of the settee. She turned to face him, and in a single fluid movement, he swept her into his arms. Nick pressed his lips to hers, running his tongue along her bottom lip before her lips parted and he massaged her tongue with his. She returned his kiss, sucking his tongue into her mouth until he groaned.

He ambled her backward towards the bedchamber, not breaking their kiss, which grew wilder by the moment. Once inside the room, he kissed her jaw and neck, nibbling at her and then soothing the nips with his tongue.

Eliza sighed, loving the man before her more than she could have thought possible. She glanced around the room and noted he had started a fire in the bedchamber as well, and there were a few candles lit on the mantle above the fireplace.

Nick took her hands in his and leaned back to look at her. His expression was an intoxicating mixture of need and love, and with the light from fire casting shadows on his handsome face, it was an image depicted right out of one of her romance novels. His chestnut hair was almost black in the low lighting and the candlelight hit his green eyes just perfectly so that they shone like a precious gem. She lost her heart to him all over again.

"Are you certain you wish to do this?" he asked, placing a soft kiss on her jaw.

"More than anything," she replied. They had talked about waiting until they were married, but the desire to be with him had consumed her. She couldn't wait for her father to approve her choice. She needed to be with him in every way, and then they would fight for their future together.

A low growl escaped his lips, and he began working the buttons of her dress, unfastening enough that he could lift it over her head and then tossed it on the chair beside the bed.

Curious about what Nick would look like without his clothing, she unbuttoned the coat he wore and pushed it off his shoulders until it fell to the floor. She worked the buttons of his white shirt next. He remained still and allowed her to do as she wished, staring into her eyes as she undid each button and freed him from his shirt.

Her breath caught when she saw his muscular chest with a light smattering of dark hair. When she ran her hands across chiseled muscles and over his shoulders, he sucked in a breath, and the nerves she had about coupling with him evaporated, leaving only raw desire. She kissed his chest, becoming wanton and bold with each press of her lips to his skin. She used her tongue in the same way he did against her neck, and his muscles flexed beneath her touch.

"Eliza, that feels so good."

She licked and kissed his collarbone and up his neck, finding the lobe of his ear. She sucked it into her mouth.

He grabbed her head and kissed her lips again. After a few moments of exploration with their tongues, he broke the kiss and pulled her night rail over her head, leaving her naked before him.

She watched his response to her, and the hunger in his eyes only emboldened her further.

"You are so beautiful," he said, looking from her breasts and down her body. "I must taste you."

She wasn't sure what he meant, but he clasped her bottom and lifted her onto the bed. He tenderly laid her down across the massive bed and positioned himself on his knees between her legs.

He kissed her lips, then kissed his way to her breasts. Her entire body shivered from the sensation of his powerful form hovering over her and the anticipation of what he would do. She gasped when he took one of her nipples into his mouth and began suckling her. "Nick," she cried out.

"Do you like this?" he asked, stopping what he was doing.

"Oh, yes," she replied.

He dipped his head to continue, smiling against her breast every time she moaned or sucked in a breath. When he used his hand to find her nub in the nest of curls between her legs, she moaned again.

He released her nipple and kissed his way down her stomach. He kissed lower and lower, shifting himself further down on the bed until his head was between her legs.

"What are you—" She cried out when his tongue flicked her pearl. "God, yes," she moaned.

He stopped and glanced up at her, a smirk playing on his lips. "Does that mean you wish for me to continue?"

"I may never wish for you to stop."

He gave a smug laugh and flicked her pearl again before circling it with his tongue. He inserted a finger into her core and moved it in and out. Her hands flew to his head, and she undulated against his mouth and hand.

She approached a release similar to the one he gave her a couple of nights ago with his hand, but this was different. Far more intense and wicked. When she tipped over the edge of her climax, she rocked and moaned, calling out his name.

He shifted himself on top of her and kissed her lips. She tasted herself on his tongue and licked the wetness off his lips. It was erotic and exhilarating, and she knew that once would never be enough.

"I could drink from you all day," he said.

"I may wish for you to do just that." She giggled when he laughed at her declaration. "I didn't know such a thing was possible," she said.

He kissed her again. "Would you like to stop now, or would you like for me to show you more?"

"I want more," she replied, the need evident in her tone. "Please, Nick."

Nick climbed off the bed and stood beside it, looking at her.

"Where are you going?" she asked, curving her lips in a playful pout.

"I must remove these now," he replied, working the buttons of his falls, his eyes not leaving hers. He pushed his breeches down to the floor and his member sprang to life, protruding from a nest of dark curls. Her gaze fixed on it, curious about what it might feel like in her hand.

He climbed back onto the bed and hovered over her, placing another sweet kiss on her lips.

"I want to touch you," she said, reaching between them to grasp the rod that stood erect between them.

He sucked in a large breath and closed his eyes when her hand closed around it. Balancing himself with one hand and his knees, he reached his free hand between them and wrapped it around hers. His cock was smooth to the touch but hard as steel.

"You can stroke me like this." He moved her hand with his, and she loved the power she felt from giving him pleasure the way he did for her.

She continued to stroke him for a few moments before he pulled her hand away. "I will spend if you should continue, and I would much rather do so after I make you come on my cock."

She bit her lip, enjoying his wicked words. "Tell me what you are going to do and don't be polite about it."

He slipped his hand between them and slid two fingers inside of her. "I'm going to replace my fingers with the head of my aching shaft, and then I'm going to move like this"—he slid his fingers in and out—"until you shatter and moan in my arms."

She released a sound that was a mixture of a sign and a moan. He pressed his lips to her ear. "Do you want me inside you now?" he whispered.

She nodded.

"Tell me you want me to make love to you with my needy cock," he said, kissing along her jaw.

"I want your cock, Nick," she whispered. "Make love to me. Now."

He withdrew his fingers and positioned himself at her opening. "This may hurt but not for long, and it shouldn't do so ever again."

He pushed himself into her with care, inch by inch. She gasped from the slight twinge of pain when he had his entire length inside of her.

"Are you all right?" he asked.

"Yes," she whispered, the pain subsiding, and she had the urge to move against him. "It doesn't hurt any longer."

He withdrew and then thrust back inside of her, causing her to see stars. She had never imagined such a pleasure and reveled in the intimacy from the man she loved most in the world filling her, the two of them joining as one. Nothing and no one else mattered but the two of them. He did it again, and she cried out.

"That's it, my love. Moan as loud as you wish. It drives me wild to hear you do so."

With every moan, he thrust deeper and harder inside of her. She wrapped her legs around him, and it became even more intense when he entered her as far as he could. He panted and groaned, and she pushed herself against him to meet his thrusts.

"You are mine," he said, thrusting hard and deep.

She responded with a loud moan and dug her fingers into his back.

"Say it," he whispered against her lips.

Eliza kissed him and broke the kiss to speak. "I am yours," she said. "I shall always be yours."

He thrust into her harder and faster.

"Oh, yes," she cried out. "Just like that. Don't stop." With each movement, she neared ever closer to madness and ecstasy. "Nick," she moaned.

He didn't relent and made good on his promise to make her shatter. When she did, she cried out his name again and bucked beneath him, arching her back. Once she rode every wave of the intense pleasure from her climax, he withdrew, his breath ragged. "God, Eliza," he groaned before warm liquid pooled on her stomach.

After a few moments, Nick climbed from the bed and removed a handkerchief from his pocket. He wiped between her legs, then her stomach, and set the handkerchief on the table beside the bed.

"I wiped away the blood, but you may be sore tomorrow. A warm bath should help," he said, settling in next to her and pulling her into his arms.

"That was more wonderful than I imagined," she said, brushing his hair away from his face. "I hope it was the same for you."

He pulled her tighter against him. "My love, I have never experienced anything as intense as being with you. I fear I am addicted to you and shall never get enough."

She giggled beside him. "Is that so?"

"It's perfect since you are mine," he said, kissing her forehead.

"Does that mean you shall meet me here tomorrow night and show me more?" she asked, placing a quick kiss on his chest.

"Nothing on this earth could keep me away."

# Acknowledgments

There are so many incredible people—both new and longtime ride-or-dies—who have supported me on this wild writing journey. Authors, readers, friends, family, co-workers… you know who you are. I'd list every one of you if I had a few extra pages (and a really small font). Just know this: I adore you, and I'm endlessly grateful.

**Steve:** My husband, tech wizard, idea bouncer, chef, laundry hero, and all-around MVP. You believe in my big, bold dreams even when they sound like total chaos. Thank you for being my partner in every possible way. Love you, babe.

**Dexter and Felix:** My boys, my chaos gremlins, and the source of many laughs. You're excellent at distracting me mid-sentence, but you're also the inspiration behind some of the snarky sibling banter that sneaks into my books. One day you'll realize your mom writes smut... and I'll probably owe you both ice cream and therapy. Love you forever.

**Rachel, Nina & Brittany:** My mom, aunt, and sister—aka my built-in cheer squad. You've supported me through every high, low, and harebrained idea I've ever chased. You hold all my most embarrassing stories, so let's make sure you never talk to anyone without legal counsel present. I love you all dearly.

**Erin:** From the moment fate brought us together in the most unexpected way, we knew we were meant to be besties. Thank you for listening to every rant, dream, plot twist in life, and meltdown—and for always helping me find my way back to joy and clarity. You're pure magic.

**Courtney:** Fate handed me a twin flame in the author world. We literally finish each other's sentences (or just say the same thing) and have become legit besties. I can't wait for the day we meet in person. Thank you for our pretty much all day, every day chats, late-night idea storms, the pep talks, and all the chaos we've embraced together. We've got this, twinsie!

**Morgan:** The magic behind the scenes! You keep everything running, offer genius-level input, and somehow make it all feel easier and more fun. This book—and honestly, this business—wouldn't be the same without you. Thank you, thank you, thank you.

**Bliss:** Who knew a smutty follow train on Insta would bring me one of my dearest friendsies? Thank you for the endless texts, laughter, spicy scene brainstorming, feedback on my chaos, and all-around moral support. So lucky we found each other!

**Rachel:** You've read just about everything I've ever written, cheered me on, and gotten delightfully deep into this universe. Thank you for your thoughtful feedback and unwavering encouragement. So happy to have you on this journey.

To my **ARC and Street Team**: Your love, feedback, and support make my heart full. Thank you for shouting about these stories from the rooftops—you make this adventure feel like a party I never want to leave.

To **Dragonblade Publishing**: Thank you for believing in me and my words. I'm so excited to grow alongside such a passionate and supportive team, and be among your esteemed group of authors.

And to all the amazing **author friends** and **influencers** I've met through social media: You're one of the best, most unexpected blessings of this entire journey. Thank you for the inspiration, the laughs, the advice—and most of all, for welcoming me into this magical community.

# About the Author

Christina Diane is an award-winning, bestselling author who loves to write super spicy, fast paced stories for the modern reader in the genres of historical romance and dark romance. Her historical romances are all set in the Regency era, with creative liberty taken within the historical setting to create a passionate, hot, intriguing story. Across all of her works, if you love combinations of high spice, witty banter, spirited heroines, forbidden romances, darker themes, and hot alpha men…then you are in for a treat! Because bad boys never go out of style!

She is a hybrid indie and traditionally published author with Dragonblade Publishing, Romance Cafe, and And You Press. She reads mostly spicy Regency romances and all shades of dark romances, as well as thrillers.

Christina lives in Northern Maine with her husband and two boys. Her family also includes their three French bulldogs who go everywhere with them, as well as two solid black cats. The entire family is always up for new adventures. When she is not writing or chasing after her family, she usually has a Kindle in her hand!

Her writing journey began at the age of nine when she created her own comic strip, Grizzly Grouch. In adulthood, she was a freelance writer for several years, mostly writing lifestyle pieces for blogs. She found that she couldn't stop thinking about stories and characters, so much that she had to get them on the page! Christina frequently has dreams of random character ARCs that go into a massive list of planned writings. She currently has more than ten series just waiting to be written!

Aside from her family, writing, and books, she loves Bridgerton, the Grinch, Jessica Rabbit, horror movies, Chucky dolls, cold brew, yoga, Hamilton, the color pink, and speaking in obscure quotes from movies and TV shows.

Christina loves chatting with her readers and talking about great reads, so please contact her on socials! She'd love to hear what you think about her books and what you'd love to see more of!